"I think this house is perfect for both of you," Olivia said. "You can build a deck in front and enjoy your meals with friends."

"Would you come if we invited you, Olivia?"

"Of course." The way he was watching her sent a tiny thrill up her spine, but it also triggered wariness. She didn't belong here, yet his words created an irresistible picture.

"And I could put up Christmas decorations outside."

"You can do whatever you want. It's your land and it will be your home."

"Home," Gabe whispered. "It's been a long time since I had that. I don't think I'd have done this without you. I don't know how we'll ever repay you."

"Just be happy. Enjoy your home and Eli. That's payment enough." Her total focus was on Gabe, on how she'd only have to balance forward on her tiptoes to touch his cheek with her lips.

Been that route before, her brain warned. *Remember the pain.*

Olivia knew lots about Gabe, including *his* painful past. Which was why Gabe wasn't interested in her as anything other than a friend.

That was what Olivia wanted, too.

Wasn't it?

Lois Richer loves traveling, swimming and quilting, but mostly she loves writing stories that show God's boundless love for His precious children. As she says, "His love never changes or gives up. It's always waiting for me. My stories feature imperfect characters learning that love doesn't mean attaining perfection. Love is about keeping on keeping on." You can contact Lois via email, loisricher@gmail.com, or on Facebook (loisricherauthor).

Books by Lois Richer

Love Inspired

Rocky Mountain Haven

Meant-to-Be Baby
Mistletoe Twins
Rocky Mountain Daddy

Wranglers Ranch

The Rancher's Family Wish
Her Christmas Family Wish
The Cowboy's Easter Family Wish
The Twins' Family Wish

Family Ties

A Dad for Her Twins
Rancher Daddy
Gift-Wrapped Family
Accidental Dad

Visit the Author Profile page at Harlequin.com for more titles.

Rocky Mountain Daddy

Lois Richer

Recycling programs
for this product may
not exist in your area.

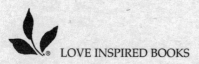

LOVE INSPIRED BOOKS

ISBN-13: 978-1-335-47910-5

Rocky Mountain Daddy

Copyright © 2019 by Lois M. Richer

www.Harlequin.com

Printed in U.S.A.

What time I am afraid, I will trust in thee.
—*Psalms* 56:3

For Mom, who wrote her last chapter so well.

And for Oliver, who's just begun his own story.

Chapter One

One minute Olivia DeWitt was happily steering her car up the hill toward home, the next minute she was heading for the ditch.

With a gasp of dismay she slammed on her brakes, managing to stay on the road shoulder—barely. She exhaled, slowly released her fingers from the wheel and then exited the car. The sight of the shredded tire made her groan.

"You couldn't have waited ten minutes before blowing?" Shielding her eyes, Olivia peered longingly at—was it still home?—The Haven, a massive stone house perched on the rocky mountain promontory above her. "At least it's summer," she consoled herself, then mocked the sentiment as a teasing breeze reminded her that June in the Canadian Rockies bore no resemblance to June in the eastern provinces.

For a microsecond Olivia considered calling The Haven and asking Jake, her foster aunts' handyman, to come and help her. Until a glance at her phone showed it was dead. Again. Not that it mattered, because she had no intention of calling.

Olivia never took the easy way out. She prided herself on being responsible and that included fixing a tire, even though she'd have to completely unpack her fully laden car to retrieve her spare.

"Nothing good comes easily," she reminded herself with a weary sigh.

Olivia had her hand on the trunk latch when a rumble to her right made her pause. A half-ton truck beetled toward her, leaving behind a massive dust plume from the bumpy dirt track—well, you could hardly call it a road.

Some might say you could hardly call the vehicle a truck. Rusted-out fenders, splotches of turquoise paint dabbed here and there—probably to contain the rust— and a cracked windshield numbered among its less noteworthy features.

"At least *his* vehicle is running," she chastised herself.

He was Gabe Webber, foreman of the Double M, the sprawling ranch next door to The Haven. Olivia knew him, but only casually. Gabe had been employed after she and her foster sisters Victoria, Adele and Gemma had left The Haven to attend university.

Years ago, when they were not quite teens, Olivia and the other girls had been brought here by Tillie and Margaret Spenser, former missionaries and aging owners of the huge stone house and pristinely forested estate known as The Haven. Despite their being dubbed *troublemakers* in the foster care system, the four girls had bonded while the Spenser sisters, whom they affectionately called "the aunties," sheltered and lovingly raised them as if they were all part of one big family. Those precious years had created a debt none of the four girls could ever hope to repay.

Over a year ago the aunties had come up with a plan to sponsor an outreach program at The Haven, a way to offer respite to troubled foster children. Victoria had set that plan into motion. Then last fall, Adele, Olivia's second foster sister, came on board as the food and beverage manager. In a recent phone call to Olivia, Victoria had raved that the foster kids who now came to The Haven on a weekend, or for weeklong programs, loved the addition of trail rides to their activities, and she'd given a big part of the credit to the Double M foreman, Gabe.

Olivia was happy for Victoria and Adele and The Haven's success, but she didn't intend to become part of it. Olivia didn't do responsibility for kids. Never again.

Gabe's battered truck pulled up behind her car, motor purring smoothly. He climbed out. Six feet four inches and leaner than lean, Gabe Webber was always the image that came to mind when Olivia thought "cowboy." Handsome and hunky, his crisp dark hair glistened in the sunshine as he whipped off his black Stetson and smiled at her.

"Hello, Olivia. Nice to see you. Having trouble?" he asked in a low rumbly voice.

Funny that she'd never noticed how deep his voice was.

"Hi, Gabe." Olivia glanced at him and then quickly away, lifting one hand to make sure her hair covered her scarred cheek. Gabe had seen the scar before, of course, and never once had he made her feel uncomfortable about it, but her actions stemmed from a lifelong habit.

"My tire blew," she explained. "I was about to dig out the spare."

"I see that. I hear you're making a move to Edmonton." Gabe assessed the damage, running one gloved fingertip over the shredded tire. "Starting a new job, your aunts said?"

"That's the plan," Olivia agreed. "I need to find an apartment and get settled in before I start work, but first I wanted to stop by The Haven and see everyone."

"Organizing people, is that what you do?" Gabe clapped on his Stetson, then shoved it to the back of his head, sky-blue eyes darkening as he studied her nod.

"Sort of. My official title was systems analyst, but the job was more about being an administrative assistant to a colonel." She shrugged. "I was tasked with making his office run more efficiently." *Too much information, Olivia.*

"Uh-huh." Gabe blinked. "Been a long time since you were here, Liv. Your Aunt Tillie and Aunt Margaret miss you." His intense gaze shifted to scrutinize the other tires. Bald tires.

"I miss my aunties, too, but it wasn't always easy to get here from Ottawa," she defended. *Please don't say I should have bought new tires.* She'd used a hefty chunk of her precious savings to store her furniture and fund her move far away from the man to whom she'd given her heart, the one who'd lied about loving her. Edmonton would be her fresh start. "How've you been, Gabe?"

"Busy. Since the Double M started offering trail rides, Victoria keeps us hopping." His droll, dry comment didn't tell Olivia he was joking, but his slow, easy smile did. "I make time to come over to The Haven every week on Fridays, though. Doughnut afternoons." Gabe licked his full lips and grinned, white teeth blazing against his tanned skin. "Chef Adele makes the best glazed doughnuts. Besides, I enjoy her kids. Those twins are quite a pair."

"Yes, they are." Olivia barely knew her adopted niece and nephew, Francie and Franklyn, but that was by choice. If she didn't get too close to them, she couldn't wreck their worlds as she'd done to other kids. She pushed up her sleeves. "I guess I'd better change—"

Her words were cut short by the squeal of tires as a dusty white SUV barreled off the highway and around the corner. It slid to a halt mere inches from Olivia's back bumper. She and Gabe both stared as a woman got out and marched toward them.

"Lady, you have to slow down around here. There could be a horse wandering in the road and if you hit it, you'd be in trouble and so would it." Gabe sounded irritated, which Olivia thought was odd for what she'd always thought such an easygoing guy. But then this cowboy loved horses as much as other people loved their kids.

The woman seemed unfazed. "I'm looking for a Gabriel Webber."

"You found him." Gabe frowned at her. "What can I—?"

The words died on his lips as the woman racewalked around the front of her vehicle to the passenger side. She yanked open the back door and a moment later dragged forward a small boy and an equally small battered suitcase.

"This is your son, Eli," she announced.

"I'm sorry, lady, you've got the wrong guy." Gabe began shaking his head, but the woman interrupted.

"Eve's son. Your son." She stared at him hard. "Eli's almost six."

Olivia's head had been swiveling back and forth between them, trying to figure out what was happening.

At the word *Eve*, Gabe stiffened, but at the word *six* his face seemed to freeze.

"Impossible," he finally whispered, blanching.

"Possible." The woman nodded. "I'm Eve's sister, Kathy Kane. We've never met, though we might have if you'd had a proper wedding instead of dragging my sister to some unsavory elopement and then dumping her when she got pregnant." When she received no response to her angry criticism she continued. "I live in Calgary now. Where Eve lived."

"Lived?" Gabe squinted at her. His face tightened into a mask, giving away nothing. He glanced at the boy again. "She's not living there now?"

"Eve died a month ago. She had cancer."

Olivia knew less than nothing about raising kids, but she immediately knew it wasn't right that the woman said the words so baldly, without even a hand on the shoulder to comfort the boy. And yet, Eli seemed untouched by the remark about his mother's passing. He just stood where he was, staring at the ground, his little face pinched and sad.

"I'm sorry," Gabe murmured.

"Me, too. She left a mess behind." Kathy Kane was not a soft-spoken woman; nor did she make any effort to conceal her irritation. "I'll clean it up. But I can't stay and talk. I've got two kids at home and the neighbor will only watch them for a while longer. I've got to go. Wait." She went back to the car.

For a moment Olivia thought Gabe feared she'd leave because he leaned forward as if he'd go after her. But Kathy returned quickly, carrying a huge handbag into which she dug furtively for a few moments before producing a bedraggled envelope.

"Eve left you this. It'll explain everything. I wrote my information on the back, just in case you need to contact me, though I'd rather you didn't. I've done enough." She stepped forward, thrust the envelope at Gabe, her jaw tight. "Don't bring him back," she growled, her voice low and threatening. "I can't keep him. I got enough trouble raising my own kids and paying all Eve's bills."

"But—"

"You be good," Kathy said to Eli, her fingers clutching his shoulder.

Olivia saw the boy wince.

"This is your dad. You're gonna live with him, like we talked about. Bye." Without another word or even an embrace, Kathy wheeled around, climbed into her car and roared back to the corner. She disappeared down the highway.

Olivia remained silent, embarrassed that she'd witnessed the incident. Gabe's frigid expression kept her from offering her sympathy, but then as he studied Eli, his icy appearance began to melt and soften. Longing filled his blue eyes—as if he couldn't quite believe his dreams had just come true. Several long moments stretched until finally Gabe walked up to the boy and squatted in front of him.

"Hello, Eli. I'm very pleased to meet you. My name is Gabe Webber." He held out a hand, withdrew it quickly to strip off his leather work glove, then thrust it out again and waited.

Olivia caught her breath when Eli looked up, staring into intense blue eyes that were an exact replica of his own. Their jutting chins had the same hard line. Dark crisp curls flopped onto prominent brows in an identical manner. The child was a mirror image of Gabe. There could be no doubt that man and boy were related.

"Are you really my dad?" Eli's murmur barely carried over the freshening wind whispering across the foothill grasses.

"That's what your aunt said." Gabe let his unshaken hand drop. "I'll have to read your mom's letter before I know more." He gulped, then added very quietly, "But I guess I am your father, Eli."

Big fat tears began to course down Eli's cheeks. His shoulders sagged.

"Why didn't you come?" he asked, his voice breaking on a sob. "I prayed and prayed. Why didn't you come?"

Then, like a broken reed that just couldn't hold itself up anymore, the little boy collapsed in a heap, sobbing his heart out.

He had a son.

Gabe stared at Eli while his brain mentally regressed to the day he'd handed Eve a copy of their divorce decree. He could still hear her voice.

You'll be sorry, Gabe.

No, Eve. I won't. I wish our marriage could have worked out, because I loved you. But you don't want me. You only ever wanted what Dad's ranch could give you—money. Now you have it, though the stress and pain you've caused us will cost us a lot more than those few dollars you grabbed at. Goodbye, Eve.

Then he'd waited for her to leave. Had she already known she was pregnant?

"Gabe?" Olivia's soft voice cracked the mirror of his past. She moved closer to meet his gaze, her silver-gray eyes clouded as she glanced pointedly at the sobbing child. "Do something," she whispered.

"I don't know—" He spread his hands helplessly. The kid wouldn't even shake his hand. What was he supposed to do?

"Oh, for mercy's—" Obviously exasperated, she walked to Eli and squatted in front of him. "Eli? My name is Olivia DeWitt. My aunties live in that great big house up there. See it?"

Eli paused in his weeping, looked up and nodded with a sniff.

"It's called The Haven," Olivia continued. "My sister is making doughnuts there today. Would you like to go with me and have some?"

Gabe stared. He hadn't seen Olivia interact with kids much. She always seemed aloof, or perhaps *standoffish* was more accurate. Yet here she was offering to take his son—*his son?*—for doughnuts. Just another thing his brain couldn't seem to process.

"The thing is, Eli, my car has a flat tire. We'll have to ride up there with Gabe in his truck. Okay?" she asked.

"Uh-huh." Eli scrubbed away the tears, which left dirt streaks across his face. He stared at Gabe. "Is he my dad for sure?" he whispered.

"I don't know, but why don't we forget about that for now and go enjoy the doughnuts. Maybe some lemonade, too. Deal?" Olivia held out a hand and, to Gabe's shock, Eli shook it.

They rose together. To Gabe it was as if some invisible bond stretched between them. A bond he hadn't been able to achieve. That stung.

"Could you drive us, please, Gabe?" Olivia asked,

locking up her vehicle. "I'll leave my car here for now. Gabe?" she prodded when he didn't respond.

"What? Uh, drive. Sure." He could hardly tear his gaze away from the boy. His son.

God, I'm going to need some help here.

He put Eli's small shabby suitcase in the truck bed without saying anything more, mostly because he couldn't think of anything appropriate. And yet, as he drove to The Haven, a million questions rolled inside his head. *Why?* That was the most pressing of them all. It seemed that his questions, like Eve's letter in his pocket, would have to wait till later.

Eve. Every nerve in Gabe's body tensed. Anger surged and the knot in his stomach tightened. *Deceiver. Cheater. Liar.* She'd been all of those, so why was he surprised by this? He clenched his jaw, braking a little harder than he should have in front of the huge stone house.

"Livvie!" Tillie and Margaret Spenser jumped up from the shaded cedar bench outside the back door. Both rushed toward them as Gabe parked and walked around to open Olivia's door.

"Another of our dear girls is home," Aunt Tillie gushed.

"Just for a week," Olivia said as she released Gabe's helping hand.

He thought that sounded like a warning.

"But—"

"My dear aunties, Victoria, and Adele have made their lives at The Haven and I'm very happy for them and you." Olivia interrupted Margaret as she hugged her close. "But Gemma and I are still the family's wanderers. I'm home for a visit, then I'll have to leave here to start my job. But having two of your four foster daughters living here permanently isn't bad, is it?" she teased.

"It's wonderful. All part of our God's glorious plan, my dear. Where's your car?" Tillie Spenser asked as she followed her sister in hugging Olivia.

"Bottom of the hill. Blown tire."

Olivia's unconcealed chagrin made Gabe smile, until Tillie released her and included him in the hugfest. Then she bent to study Eli.

"Hello, young man. Welcome to The Haven. It's doughnut day, did you know that?"

"She said," Eli responded, shooting a small smile at Olivia. The smile disappeared when he looked at Gabe.

"This is Eli," Olivia explained. "He'll be joining us," she managed to say just before being encircled by Adele's adopted twins, Francie and Franklyn, who'd come racing around the side of the house.

Gabe noted how quickly Olivia drew away from them.

"Hey, guys, you're kinda dirty," she said, nose wrinkling at the muddy streaks on her formerly pristine white shirt.

"Yeah. Choc'late mud pies." Francie grinned. "We gotta wash 'fore we c'n eat doughnuts," she told Eli.

"It's a rule," Franklyn agreed.

Gabe had loved the twins from the moment Adele arrived with them over six months ago. He couldn't have been happier when she'd married his boss, Mac McDowell, owner of the Double M, because it meant the cute pair now lived on the ranch. He loved kids, had always wanted some of his own, but Eve—*don't go there.*

He had a son. Gabe couldn't make that sink into his

brain. Nor could he comprehend why Eve hadn't told him, especially after she'd become ill.

"Come on." Francie grabbed Eli's hand. "Washup time. An' don't miss no dirt 'cause we can't eat nothin' till we get clean an' the doughnuts are yummy." She whirled to inspect the adults. "Uncle Gabe, you got dust on your cheek. You gotta wash, too."

"Yup, you do," Franklyn agreed. He grabbed Eli's other hand and drew him alongside, discussing crash-up cars. Eli went along with a confused look on his face.

"Let's do have some doughnuts," Aunt Margaret said. She and her sister followed the kids inside. Only Gabe and Olivia remained.

"I figured you wouldn't want to explain to them about Eli until you have everything sorted out," she said quietly.

"Thanks." He could feel her questions.

"I didn't know you'd been married, Gabe."

"At eighteen. For about three years." Because she'd witnessed the debacle with Kathy, Gabe figured he owed Olivia at least a rudimentary explanation. "Eve was the new girl in town and I fell hard for her. My dad didn't approve, though. We eloped, then she moved onto our ranch. I'd worked the ranch with Dad my whole life and I loved it, but Eve said it was boring and hated it. She started to cause problems—on the ranch and between Dad and me. I finally realized that when she looked at me, all she saw was a meal ticket."

"I'm sorry," she whispered.

"Me, too." He pursed his lips. Best to get it said and then forget it. As if! "Eve wanted out, so Dad agreed to sell off part of our land to pay her off. She took the money and ran, but Dad's treasure, our ranch, was decimated. We couldn't ranch on so little land, though he fought hard to make it work. Six months later he died from a massive coronary. I had to sell the land at rock-bottom prices."

"Oh, no." Olivia sounded genuinely upset. "What did you do then?"

"Enlisted. Did two tours, but I hated it. I worked at Wranglers Ranch in Tucson for a while. Tried to rebuild my faith in God." He heaved a sigh. "Then I got into equine-assisted learning. Eventually I came to the Double M and—" He shrugged. "That's my story. My stupidity in marrying Eve cost me my dad and my home."

"I'm so sorry. You never saw Eve again?"

"No. And I never wanted to," he muttered, tension building in his head. "Until today," he grated.

"You never fell in love again?" Olivia's hand went up in the automatic way she had of smoothing her hair over her damaged cheek. Funny, but unless she drew attention to it, Gabe never even noticed her scar.

"No." Even now, memories of that youthful over-the-top love and the gut-wrenching pain of knowing it wasn't reciprocated burned inside. "Eve ended my dreams of love and family. I grew up fast and I gave up dreaming." The words emerged sounding bitter. But then he had a right to be bitter, even more so now.

Why didn't you tell me we have a son, Eve?

"And that's enough for you?" she asked, a frown marring her beauty.

"I have a good job with horses, which I love. I live in a great community and I get to be part of The Haven's ministry. Someday I'd like to have my own spread, but…" He shrugged. "Really, why do I need a house and land?"

"I'm sorry, Gabe." Olivia's softly voiced words offered comfort, but he wouldn't take it.

"So am I. My stupidity in marrying Eve killed my dad. I'll never forgive her for that." Why had he told Olivia that? What good did it do? Out of the corner of his eye he saw Eli standing in the doorway. Surely the boy hadn't overheard his snarky comment? "Let's go enjoy those doughnuts," he said with forced cheerfulness.

"Wait." She stepped forward to rub the dust from his cheek. "Now the twins will allow you to eat doughnuts," Olivia said with a grin.

Truth be told, Gabe wasn't sure he could swallow anything right now. What he desperately wanted was to lose himself in the forest surrounding them and read the letter that burned a hole in his shirt pocket.

Later, he promised himself grimly. He'd read Eve's paltry excuses for keeping his son a secret later.

Chapter Two

"Is Eli staying here?" Victoria asked Olivia later that afternoon.

Olivia sat on the deck beside her sister, basking in the warmth of the sun, shielded from any breeze by The Haven.

"Not that he isn't welcome," Victoria backtracked. "Everyone's welcome at The Haven. But the aunties have some guests arriving tomorrow..."

"I don't have any answers, Vic." Olivia knew her sister's frown meant she'd demand some explanation, so she relayed the events of Eli's arrival.

"Gabe's a daddy?" Victoria grinned. "Couldn't happen to a nicer guy. He's great with kids."

"Well, he sure doesn't seem to know what to do with Eli." Olivia remembered the devastated look on the cowboy's face when Eli hadn't shaken his hand. Then she remembered Eli's pitiful sob. "There's something going on with that child, though I'm not sure what that is."

Victoria's adopted son, Mikey, was playing with Francie and Franklyn on the jungle gym equipment about six feet away. Eli stood apart, watching them.

"Probably after such a loss it will take him a while to feel his way. Most kids are like that." Vic smiled at her daughter, Grace, who was learning to walk. "Don't worry. Gabe will make him feel welcome. Meanwhile, your timing in coming home couldn't be better."

"Why?" There was a note in her sister's voice that worried Olivia. "What's going on, Vic?"

"The aunts' lawyers and accountants are coming to check out everything at the end of the month, to make sure The Haven's outreach program complies with all government rules." Victoria winced. "The office is a mess, Livvie. It just isn't my gift," she defended herself when Olivia frowned. "I can never seem to get the paper under control. I've been late filing a couple of forms, too." Her head drooped.

"I'll take a look." Olivia smiled at her sister's relief. "Why didn't you hire an assistant?"

"I did. She made things worse. Triple booked us at Easter. Forgot to mention she'd confirmed four military visitors were coming when we were already full. Can you say *nightmare*?" Victoria rolled her eyes.

"I'll set up some better systems, see if that— Hey, where's he going?"

"Who?" Victoria tracked her gaze. "Gabe? He has eyes like a hawk. Probably sees something down there. Maybe I'd better take a look." She lifted Grace and stretched as if to hand her over, but Olivia didn't move. She couldn't take her niece because warning bells filled her head.

"Leave Gabe, Vic. Eli's aunt gave him a letter from his ex. I'm guessing the poor guy needs a few moments to read it and figure out what's what." Olivia couldn't stop herself from chucking the darling little girl under the chin. "Miss Grace looks like Ben."

"Good. My husband is very handsome." Vic frowned. "Still have your aversion to kids, huh, Liv?" she asked sympathetically.

"It's not an aversion. How could anyone have an aversion to this sweetheart?" Heart aching, Olivia smiled at Grace and then sighed, knowing she wasn't fooling Victoria. "It's pure fear and you know it. I'm terrified to be responsible for any kid."

"Because of what happened years ago when you babysat in those foster homes." Victoria covered Olivia's hand. "Sweetie, the kid that died in the fire—you were too young to be looking after anybody back then, and his death was an accident. The child that drowned—that didn't happen because of anything you did, either."

Vic had pried the truth of Olivia's ugly past out of her when they were fourteen.

"But I was in charge—"

"The point is, you shouldn't have been, Liv. The authorities even said so. You were a strong, competent and responsible kid, yes, but you weren't the adult in that home. Those parents were wrong to blame you. *They* should have been watching their kid *and* you *and* the pool. It wasn't fair to expect you to be in charge. The fire was an accident and it was not your fault." Vic patted her shoulder.

"Maybe. But it doesn't change anything inside my head, Vic. Caring for kids, being responsible for them still terrifies me." Olivia rose, uneasy with those awful memories and unwilling to revisit them. "It's just the way I am. Sorry." She made a face at Grace, who only giggled.

"But to keep avoiding children means this fear robs you… Livvie, don't you want to have your own children someday?"

"No!" Seeing that her sharp response had drawn frowns from the kids, Olivia smiled at them reassuringly before resuming her seat. She wasn't going to tell Vic about Martin or that she'd given up on marriage because he'd pretended he wanted to marry her even though he was already married to and living with someone else. *Betrayer.* "I just want to start my new job, prove myself and earn the things I've never had."

"Things are worth more than family?" Vic sounded disapproving.

"No, and it's not a competition. It's just—it's best for me." She shrugged, relieved to see Gabe emerge from the woods, though he wasn't alone. "Looks like he found some stragglers," she mused.

"Those two again." Victoria stood, her lips pressed tight together. "That pair has caused more than enough problems today."

"I doubt they've done anything as bad as what we did at that summer camp, before the aunties brought us here," Olivia reminded. "We four girls terrorized everyone."

"True. Think this is my payback?" With Grace in her arms, Victoria straightened her shoulders before striding forward to meet the threesome. She listened to what Gabe said, shook her head at the pair and ushered them to the meadow where they were supposed to be learning to rock climb with their group.

Olivia watched it play out, marveling at her sister's ease in handling these troubled youth. Judging by the slump of their shoulders as they walked down the path with her, the two had been strongly chastised.

"Vic's good at this job, isn't she?" Olivia murmured, her gaze now focused on Gabe. His attention seemed riveted on his son.

"Vic's like your aunts. A dragon lady lives under that big generous smile of hers." Gabe glanced at her, then back to Eli. "Any trouble?"

"With Francie and Franklyn in charge?" She rolled her eyes. "Not yet, but there will be. Did you read your letter?"

"Didn't get a chance before I found those two."

"What are you going to do about Eli?" Olivia was curious to hear his plans.

"Ask the aunts if he can stay here, I guess." He shrugged at her surprise. "I live in a bunkhouse, Olivia. There's barely room to turn around let alone fit in a kid. It never mattered before, but—"

"It does now. You need to start looking for a home." She could see the idea surprised him. "He's a little boy, Gabe. He's been pulled from the only place he knew. He needs his own home. With his father."

"What kind of a home?" He shrugged at her confused look. "I'm clueless. I've been saving for my own spread for years, but—"

"Buy it," she interrupted.

"Can't. I've never found what I want. But even if I had, I have to consider…things."

"Such as?" Why did she feel he was hesitating?

"Such as—it might be dangerous for a kid from the city to live on a ranch. Maybe a temporary place in town is better." Gabe's suddenly narrowed stare made

Olivia uncomfortable. "You wouldn't have time to help me look, would you?"

"Me?" Olivia blinked. "What do I know about finding a home for a little boy?"

"Probably more than me. It doesn't have to be right away," Gabe quickly added. "Eli could stay here for a while. Your aunts wouldn't mind. In fact, it might be better if he settled in here."

"No, it wouldn't." Olivia wasn't sure why it felt so important to get Eli into a home of his own with his father. Maybe it was because she'd sensed an inner angst in the child. Or maybe it was because at Eli's age she'd always longed to belong to someone. Or maybe it was Gabe himself.

Granted, she didn't know him well, but she'd always thought him too easygoing, too laid-back, too prepared to wait for things instead of making them happen, like staying in a bunkhouse instead of getting the spread he obviously wanted.

Kathy had said Eli was almost six. Hadn't father and son waited long enough?

"Why wouldn't it be good for him to stay here long-term?" Gabe frowned at her.

"Because though he's welcome, Eli's a visitor here. Kids need a place where they feel secure. Being shunted around, not having a permanent parent in his life, nothing to call his own—that's no way to start off your life together. That boy needs a home of his own, with you, his dad. Pronto."

"Strong feelings much?" Gabe's blue eyes twinkled. "So, you're offering to help?"

She'd fallen right into that. Olivia sighed.

"Fine. I'll help you look for a place to live, Gabe. But

that's all. I won't help you decorate it or buy furniture for it or any of that stuff." As if she had any clue as to how to make a house into a home for a cowboy and a kid. Organizing systems, creating efficiency, that was her specialty. Not helping somebody belong.

"Okay," the big cowboy agreed easily. "I can always ask salesclerks about furniture."

Oh, brother.

"This home is for you and Eli. You should make the decisions about it together. You do know I'm leaving soon, probably next week, but for sure no later than the end of June."

"When do you want to start looking? Tomorrow?" And she'd thought Gabe laid-back. "I'm off in the afternoon." He looked very eager now.

After her first glance at Eli, Olivia had wanted to help him. But she didn't do kids. Fear of the past happening again, of being responsible and failing, kept her from interacting with her own nieces and nephews. What was so different about Eli that he made her feel he needed her?

Olivia exhaled. She had no idea why this child tugged at her heart. All she knew was that she had to do what she could. And the sooner she helped Eli, the sooner she'd feel okay about leaving The Haven to get on with building her future. Alone. As usual.

Helping Gabe had nothing to do with it.

"Tomorrow afternoon is good," she agreed.

Gabe,
First, I apologize. I should have told you about Eli years ago. But you had your dad and your ranch. Eli was all I had. I guess I wanted to punish you for not making me stay with you, so I kept

the two of you apart. That was stupid and selfish. All I did was cheat my son of knowing his father, someone he's asked about since he first learned to speak. I cheated you of knowing him, too, and I'm so sorry. He's a wonderful boy, Gabe. So curious, so generous. His heart is so tender. Now he's hurting, worried that I'm dying, and he'll be left all alone.

I wish I'd eaten my pride ages ago, but now it's too late. I'm too ill to come and find you. I'm in hospice and there are days I can hardly lift my head. I can barely hug Eli, so I tell him that I love him and that one day you'll come for him. I don't know where you are, Gabe, but I pray that somehow God will bring you and our child together. God is my best friend now. You're the one who first introduced us, remember? My favorite Bible verse is, "He hath made everything beautiful in His time." God will do that with you and Eli, I know it. Forget about me and how I ruined things between us and concentrate on this wonderful little boy who needs your love so badly. He needs a dad, too, and I know you'll be a great father. Love him, Gabe.

While I've been ill I had to let my sister care for Eli, but please don't leave our son with Kathy. He has a tender soul and she'll crush him, just as she did me at that age. Contact the lawyer on the card I've included. On my death you'll receive permanent custody of Eli. I so wish I would have told you this in person, but since I can't, this is from my heart. Please, I beg you, love our son.

Even if you never forgive me, Gabe, love Eli. He desperately needs you.
Eve

Sitting on his bed in his bunkhouse that evening, Gabe reread Eve's letter several times. Every time he did, the knot of bitterness inside him wound tighter. Simple for Eve to say she was sorry. She was gone. She didn't have to face him; she'd never answer for what she'd done. But he'd lost almost six years of his son's life, six years when he could have watched Eli learn to walk, to talk, call him Daddy, share baby kisses and birthdays.

Forget the past. Focus on Eli, his logical brain ordered. Probably good advice, but Gabe doubted he could ever forget or forgive Eve for what she'd done.

So now what?

Lips pursed, he folded Eve's letter and slid it back into its envelope. He selected a new envelope and wrote Kathy's address on it. He filled out a check, signed it and slid it inside. Then he added a note. *Use this for whatever you need.* A father should be responsible for his kid's expenses. Better late than never. He sealed the envelope and set it on a shelf, ready to mail.

Eve's letter went into a small bronze box with a lid that Gabe snapped shut before shoving it into a drawer. Though the letter was hidden from his sight, it felt vividly alive in his seething brain.

Head and heart aching, Gabe went outside and sank onto the step, peering into the half-lit sky. Summer nights in the mountains never really got dark. Sunset and sunrise would meet soon. What would tomorrow hold?

"I know the thoughts that I think toward you, saith

the Lord. Thoughts of peace and not of evil, to give you an unexpected end." That verse had been Gabe's life's motto for years.

You've known about all of this for a long time, Lord. But I'm stunned, he prayed silently. *I've tried to follow You as best I can, but—a son? I never imagined—show me the best way to win his heart. Show me how to be Eli's father, Lord.*

Gabe prayed until there were no more words left. But nervous worry, concern that he'd mess up and perhaps hurt this little boy he didn't even know, plus uncertainty about his suddenly shifting world, did not abate.

His pastor's Sunday-morning sermons last winter had been all about trusting God. Gabe had been so certain he'd been doing that. But Eli's appearance today had rocked his world and shaken his faith. Almost six years—why had Eve done it? But more importantly, why had God let her? How could he trust God now?

Because a sense of futility hung over him, Gabe shifted his thoughts toward practicalities. How would he know what kind of a place to get for Eli?

Olivia's image flickered through his brain. She didn't seem to hesitate when making decisions. Maybe he could lean on her, let her take the lead in this house-hunting business. After all, she'd grown up at The Haven, certainly the best home in the area. She'd know all the things a good home should have.

The knot inside Gabe eased. Yeah, he'd follow Olivia's lead. Could it be that's why God had brought her back at this particular time? To be a friend? To help him?

Startled by awareness that he was allowing a pretty woman he barely knew to become so involved in his personal life, in direct opposition to everything he'd resolved after Eve's departure and in the years since, Gabe's brain whirled. He'd take Olivia's help, he decided, but he would not allow anything more than friendship between them, because though she was very attractive, romance wasn't for him. Never again would he let himself be that vulnerable.

When he finally retired, sleep was elusive because Gabe knew that no matter how great Olivia was at organizing things, the fact remained that Eli was not a ranch kid. He'd even shied away from Spot and Dot, the Spenser sisters' mild-tempered dogs. What would happen when the kid met a horse?

Horses were Gabe's world.

Were. But now he had a son. With whom he had nothing in common.

"This could be doable." The following day Gabe tilted back on his cowboy boot heels, surveyed the interior of the tiny rental house he'd been told about and gulped.

"You're kidding, right?" Olivia bristled with indignation. "You and Eli would have no time to spend together because you'd be constantly repairing something."

"It's a rental, Olivia," he muttered. "*They're* supposed to look after all the maintenance."

"Looks like they're doing a bang-up job," she muttered in disgust, flicking a finger against the peeling countertop, nudging a toe against a loose floorboard and obviously struggling not to inhale the overwhelming odor of too many cats. "Come on, Eli. Let's get out of here," she muttered, and headed out the door, stumbling on the faulty step.

Gabe steadied her before following to stand beside her in the long grass outside, next to Eli, who studied the tilted bilious green house with disapproval.

"That house stinks," his son said, the first words he'd spoken since he'd climbed into Gabe's truck after lunch.

"We'll clean it out," Gabe assured him, striving for a positive tone.

"Not without removing the carpets, curtains and wallpaper, which is what I like to call a gut job." Obviously repelled, Olivia strode toward the truck. "Moving on."

So they did move on. And again, several times. After the fourth house, Gabe began to lose hope in his wobbly dream of a home for his son. Olivia found problems with every single rental they viewed. Not that the problems weren't there. They were, and Gabe knew it. But he had to find a place if he was going to keep Eli with him, if he was going to be a real father.

"Can we stop for coffee, please?" Olivia licked her lips. "I need a break."

"Sure." Gabe pulled up in front of the local diner, shoved the gearshift into Park and climbed out. He reached to help Eli, but the boy veered away from him and exited on Olivia's side. It was one of several signs that Gabe interpreted to mean his son was upset with him, though he couldn't figure out exactly why that should be.

Inside Olivia chose the best booth in the place, halfway between the entrance and the kitchen with a street view. It was like her to have automatically selected the best one, Gabe thought. She seemed to possess an inner ability that almost unconsciously prioritized every decision she made. Maybe it came from her years of working for the military.

He paused to admire her in the stream of sunshine. She looked lovely. Efficiently lovely, he corrected. Her navy slacks and coordinating navy-and-white sweater set were perfect for an afternoon of house hunting. Businesslike casual, Gabe would have termed it.

As usual, her hair covered the left side of her face to fall over the scar and tuck under her jaw. For a minute he wondered about that scar and how it had gotten there. Then her glossy dark hair recaptured his attention. On the other side of her face it entwined behind her ear revealing silver-hooped earrings, a perfect complement to the two thin silver chains around her slim neck. Her rust-brown boots looked like they'd be comfortable in whatever terrain they happened upon.

"Do you want milk to drink?" she asked Eli.

"Pop." Eli didn't seem to be requesting.

Olivia glanced at Gabe. He nodded at the server and waited until Olivia ordered coffee, then requested a cup for himself.

"And a large plate of fries, please," he added.

"You're hungry already?" Olivia's eyes stretched wide. She checked the slim silver watch on her wrist. "Lunch was only an hour ago."

"Didn't get any lunch. One of the riders decided he didn't want his lesson to end." Gabe smirked. "But Betsey didn't like it when the kid dug his heels into her side and wouldn't get off. She decided his ride was over."

"What happened?" Eli blinked as if he'd surprised himself with the question.

"Betsey, uh, let him down." Gabe winked at Eli.

"She bucked him off?" Eli's eyes grew huge.

Gabe was about to launch into a full-fledged tale of the event when Olivia cleared her throat. He glanced at her. She shook her head, just once.

"The trail riding horses at the Double M don't buck off their riders. Do they?" she asked Gabe pointedly.

"Uh, no. They're way better trained than that." Gabe smiled at the boy. "Betsey just moved against the rails and rubbed so he had to let go and slide off. But he pretended he was hurt so we had to get him checked out. That was my lunch hour."

"Oh." Eli frowned as he considered that.

"Would you like to learn to ride, Eli?" Olivia smiled as their server brought their drinks and a huge plate of golden fries.

"Uh-uh. Horses are *huge*." Eli helped himself to a fry after Gabe nudged the plate toward him. "How old were you?" he asked his father.

"When I first rode a horse?" It was the first time his son had addressed him directly. Gabe tried to conceal his pleasure and treat the question matter-of-factly. "I was raised on a ranch, Eli. My dad told me he first put me on a horse when I was two. But I don't remember that," he added lest the boy feel intimated.

This fatherhood thing was treacherous. A guy had to be so careful not to say the wrong thing. What should he say next? While he thought it over, Gabe squirted ketchup on the edge of the plate and dipped his fries into it, hoping his stomach would stop that embarrassing growling. He hid his smile when Eli copied his actions by dipping into the ketchup, too.

"Not everyone rides the full-size horses, Eli. There are miniature horses at the Double M, just your size,"

Gabe explained. "Francie and Franklyn like to ride them."

Eli thought that over as he ate more fries.

"What kind of things would you like in the house you live in, Eli?" Olivia's question startled Gabe, but then he figured it was probably one he should have asked himself. Maybe the kid had preferences.

"Windows." Eli popped another fry into his mouth and chewed thoughtfully. "So I can see to draw."

"You like to draw." Olivia nodded. "I see. What else would you like?"

"Grass. Mine." Eli fell silent for a moment. The sad look he gave Olivia tore at Gabe's heart. "Not just a park."

"It's not the same, is it? I lived in an apartment in Ottawa and I loved the park, but having your own yard is way better. Did your aunt have a yard?" she asked nonchalantly.

Not nonchalantly enough, Gabe figured, watching Eli's face close like a clamshell.

"No." Eli said nothing else.

And here I've lived my life surrounded by grass. I could have... Inside Gabe the nugget of bitterness toward Eve hardened.

"Too bad." Olivia sipped her coffee. "What other things would you like, Eli?"

"Nobody beside us?" Eli peeked sideways at her, as if he doubted this could be accomplished.

"You mean no neighbors?" When he nodded, she added, "You don't like neighbors?"

"Yelling."

Was it fear that made the kid's eyes so huge? Gabe wondered.

"I don't like yelling, either. What about a pet? A cat maybe?" Olivia ignored Gabe's vigorously shaking head.

What was the woman doing? A house, a kid *and* pets? Gabe cleared his throat, but she ignored him.

"No cat," Eli said firmly.

"Okay. A dog? A horse?" she added, even though Gabe shook his head.

"A canary. I like canaries." Eli licked the ketchup off his fingers, then dug in his pocket. "Like this." His small fingers spread out a sheet of paper on the table to reveal a carefully drawn canary with even the tiny claws sketched out.

"Eli, this is beautiful." Olivia leaned nearer to study the delicate strokes. "Did you used to have a canary?"

"Aunt Kathy did. It died." The words sounded ominous.

"It's a very good drawing," Gabe said quietly. "So you like to draw birds?"

"Uh-huh." Suddenly Eli came alive. "In the house?" he said in a rushed tone.

The house, not *my* house or *our* house, Gabe noted. "Yes?"

"Could I get one of those seats in front of a window to sit and look out? An' maybe a tree?" he added wistfully. "Then when birds come an' sit in the tree, I could draw 'em. I really like drawing birds."

"We'll put that on the list." Gabe pulled out a small notebook he kept tucked in his shirt pocket. He opened it to a fresh page and dutifully noted *window seat, canary* and *tree*. "They're such small things to want," he said softly to Olivia, who was watching him.

"And such important things," she agreed with a

funny smile that half mocked, half shared. Then she said briskly, "That was great coffee. Ready to start looking again, Eli?"

"'Kay." He drank the rest of his soda, ate one more ketchup-laden fry, wiped his fingers carefully on a napkin and then slid out of the booth.

After a rest stop they were back in the truck. Gabe felt a little better about this search now that Eli finally seemed interested, but everything they saw was too small or too dirty or out of his price range.

"I'm sorry," Olivia said as she watched Eli climb back into the truck. "I guess Chokecherry Hollow is such a small town that there aren't many rentals. I should have realized that. Just for curiosity sake, let's drive past the Realtor's office and see what's in the For Sale window."

"Sure." Gabe had already checked the advertisements in the huge picture windows last night, but he pulled up to the curb anyway.

"Maybe we'll see something here that will suit," Olivia murmured.

Gabe doubted that. Most all the ads were for massive spreads with fancy homes and lots of cattle, starting well above seven figures. Way beyond his means. But he would look with her because he knew Olivia well enough now to know she'd insist they leave no stone unturned in their search. Since Eli had fallen asleep, Olivia eased free of him, stepped out of the truck and quietly closed her door. Gabe did the same. They met in front of the windows.

"I had no clue ranch land sold for this much," Olivia gasped after scanning the display, obviously taken aback by the prices.

"They're big spreads. I wouldn't be able to work at the Double M and manage so much land or cattle," Gabe told her.

"You don't want to raise your own herd?" She looked at him with those big silver-gray eyes, as if trying to fathom why he would settle for less than his own animals.

"It takes a while to build a really good herd and lots of money to cover the lean years so, no, I don't. But it's mainly because my interest has always been horses." He shrugged, adding before she could question him, "That also takes lots of cash and time to build your stock."

"I see." She turned back to survey the window once more. A long time passed before she finally faced him. "There's nothing here for us?"

Us. He liked the sound of that. As if he wasn't alone in this new and uncertain world. *But only because she's a friend*, his brain reminded.

Olivia frowned at him, waiting for a response.

Gabe simply shook his head. Together they walked to the truck. He held her door until she was inside, then gently closed it. Once he was behind the wheel again he looked at her.

"I guess that's it," he muttered.

"You're giving up already?" She glared at him, eyes shooting silver sparks. "We've only been looking for what?" She checked her watch. "Three hours. And you still need a place to live with your son. Let's go for a drive."

"A drive?" He wanted to ask why, but faced with her implacable glare, Gabe obediently shifted into gear. "Where to?"

"In the country," was her only directive.

That was fine by Gabe. He never tired of the densely verdant rolling hills, thickets of green trees, lush meadows and rocky peaks where granite foundations thrust into the light.

"It's beautiful, isn't it?" Olivia breathed reverently. "Ottawa's lovely, too, but I never realized how much I've missed all these wide-open spaces."

"Quite a Creator we have," Gabe agreed.

"Look at that house, nestled against the hillside. It has a wonderful view."

"That's the Browns' place, Evensong. Not much more than a few acres now." Sadness crept through Gabe. "They bought a big spread five years ago to live out their retirement dream, but they've been slowly selling off bits of land to neighbors. Since Mrs. Brown got sick Art just can't handle it all and look after her."

"Mavis? Isn't that her name?" Olivia smiled at his nod. "I think the aunties mentioned this morning that she's having treatment in Edmonton."

"Yeah. Would you mind if we stopped for a few minutes? I'd like to see if there's anything Art needs help with. I think he's home today to catch up."

Relieved when Olivia nodded her agreement, Gabe pulled into the yard. He usually stopped over to check the few head of cattle grazing in the pasture and sometimes curried the last two horses the Browns owned. The house looked worse than usual in the bright sunlight. It sure could use a coat of paint. Maybe he could manage that this summer. Somehow.

After he'd figured out fatherhood.

As they pulled into the yard, Art Brown emerged from the shed carrying a gas can and a wrench. To Gabe he looked weary beyond belief.

"How are you doing?" he asked after he'd introduced Olivia. Eli was still sleeping.

"Okay. Hated to leave Mavis in Edmonton alone, but she must be close to the hospital for her treatment and I've got to tend things here. All this back and forth is wearing me out," Art admitted, heaving a sigh. "But you don't want to hear my woes. Come on inside and I'll make you a cup of coffee. Place isn't very tidy but—"

"You have the most glorious deck. Do you mind if we sit out here for a bit? Then Eli, that's Gabe's son, will see us when he wakens. And we had coffee earlier so don't go to any trouble on our account." Olivia's smile seemed to put the fatigued man at ease.

"Okay. Have a seat. Son, huh? Good for you, Gabe." Art sat down gratefully. "Thought maybe I'd mow the yard today. Sure does need it, but that beast won't start." He shook his head at the ancient green ride-on mower sitting in the long grass. "Guess it's getting old, just like me."

"Mind if I take a look?" Gabe asked. He shot Olivia a questioning glance, relieved when she nodded. "Stay here and relax," he ordered Art with a grin. "I'm better if I work alone. Or at least I'm less embarrassed when I can't figure it out."

"Join my club. Have at it." Art stretched out his legs when Gabe stepped off the deck and bent to look at the mower.

"My aunts, Tillie and Margaret, send their best wishes to you and Mavis. They're praying for both of you," Olivia said quietly. "Is there anything we can do to make things easier for you?"

"Everybody's already doing so much," the man said,

tears welling at the corners of his eyes. "Embarrassing to ask for more."

"That's what friends are for," Olivia assured him.

Gabe listened in unabashedly, liking the way Olivia deflected the man's concern.

"We'd like to help if we can, Art," she said now. "Please tell us how we can best do that."

Gabe already knew most of the issues at Evensong. He'd been trying to rectify them since the couple had left, but the list seemed to increase daily.

"I'm most worried about the house roof," the retired man admitted. "God's blessed us so far this summer and we haven't had a big deluge. But the next downpour is going to cause huge problems inside." Art hung his head, obviously ashamed he hadn't been able to fix it.

"Don't you dare go up there, Arthur." Gabe called his warning loudly, hoping the older man would heed him. "Climbing on roofs won't help that knee of yours." He glanced at Olivia, surprised to see her writing in a tiny notebook. "We'll get it done," he assured his friend with a grin while wondering, *When?*

"What else needs doing, Art?" Olivia glanced around.

"Well, the cattle and the horses are a worry, of course. Gabe's been great at taking care of them while I'm gone but we can't keep relying on him. Guess I'll have to sell them, though Mavis raised that mare from a foal and she's attached to it—"

"You know I don't mind caring for the animals, Art." Gabe fiddled with the carburetor, then flicked the starter switch. The mower sputtered momentarily but finally came to life. He let it run for a few minutes as he added gas from the nearby can. "I'm going to give it a whirl," he called to the pair on the deck.

He noticed Art start to rise, saw Olivia restrain him with a gentle hand on his arm. Then, heads bent together, the two chatted and Olivia wrote some more in her book. Gabe was curious about that book, but he concentrated on grass cutting until he saw Eli's head pop up inside the cab. Then he parked the machine, got off and went to his son.

"Ever ridden on a mower?" Gabe asked. Eyes wide, Eli shook his head. "Come on, you can ride with me while we cut this grass for my friend." He explained the rules about riding to Eli, then sat him on the back of the long seat. "Hang on to me now," he ordered, a tiny rush of pleasure surging through him when the small hands wrapped around his waist.

Just then Gabe happened to glance up. Olivia was watching them. She smiled and nodded her approval. For some reason that made him unreasonably happy, and he returned to his mowing with a light heart.

Whatever You have in store for me, God, I thank You for my son and for a friend like Olivia. Underneath that reserve, she's got a good heart.

Chapter Three

Back at The Haven, Gabe accepted Tillie and Margaret's invitation for supper. He always enjoyed the camaraderie around their table and envied the easy pleasure this family took in being together, welcoming whomever joined them. Tonight Gabe especially enjoyed how Eli seemed to relax and even laugh with Victoria and Ben's adopted son, Mikey, who was about the same age. Yet Eli still avoided his father, which bugged Gabe no end.

"Where's Francie and Franklyn?" Eli asked.

"At home on the Double M where they live. Saturday night is pizza night at their house. Then they go on a family ride. Francie and Franklyn ride their miniature horses, and Adele and Mac ride on the big horses." Victoria glanced from Olivia to Gabe. "What did you three do today?"

Gabe let Olivia explain about their house search and the subsequent visit to Art.

"There are one or two ways we could help there, aunties," she ended quietly.

"We'd love that. Art and Mavis have become very

dear souls in our community. Tell us what they need, Livvie," Tillie demanded, leaning forward.

Victoria got the boys busy with a board game while Olivia consulted her notes and then spoke, astounding Gabe with her perception and quick assessment of the situation.

"Eli needed the bathroom so I took him inside Art's house and noticed the house needs a cleaning. With all the outside work, I don't suppose Art's had much time or energy. When Mavis comes home, I'm sure cleaning will be the last thing on her mind as she recuperates."

"We'll have a cleaning bee. We love bees, but our ladies' group hasn't had one in forever." Tillie beamed. "We'll go Monday morning. I know Art plans on returning to Edmonton tomorrow, so we won't upset his plans. Done."

"Next?" Margaret, not to be outdone by her sister's enthusiasm, waited impatiently.

"Well." Olivia glanced at Gabe as if to ask his opinion.

"You're doing fine," he assured her.

"It's just—" She glanced at her list, then around the table. "The way Art spoke about Mavis and their stay in the city made me think neither of them are eating properly. I doubt if she's well enough to cook and he said he can't, so perhaps a few frozen meals would be in order?"

"Adele has plenty of them in the freezer. Tillie and I will deliver some this evening. Art can take them with him to Edmonton." Margaret smiled. "Good thinking, Livvie." The Spenser sisters smiled at each other, but those smiles faded when Olivia cleared her throat.

"I wasn't finished." Her cheeks pinked when everyone looked at her in surprise. "The place needs a second work bee."

"For?" Margaret was busily making her own list.

"The outside. Art mentioned the roof leaks. Gabe warned him to stay off the roof because of his knee, but apparently it must be fixed before the next rain or considerable damage will occur inside." Olivia looked around the table. "Their hardwood floors are lovely. It would be a shame for rain leaks to ruin them."

Gabe had noticed those gorgeous floors many times, but he hadn't given a thought to their shape if a leaky roof damaged them. Full marks to Olivia the organizer.

"Our men's group from the church can reroof the house. We have the cash to pay for it and we've been looking for a way to use those funds locally." Ben, Victoria's husband, mused aloud. "It's not a large house so it shouldn't take long. I'll ask the guys, see if Tuesday works."

"That's more than generous." Olivia noted his offer in her book before inhaling. "Then there's the painting," she added in a rush.

"Painting?" Tillie leaned forward. "Inside, you mean?"

"It could certainly use a refresh inside, but I was thinking more of the outside. The siding is peeling and looks so shabby. It would be disheartening for Mavis to come home to."

"I've been meaning to paint the house," Gabe admitted, "but I never gave a thought to Mavis's feelings." He smiled at Olivia. "Your perceptions intrigue me."

"I like organizing things in a way that makes sense to those who'll be using them." She shrugged. "It's what I do—did. Will do, in my new job."

"It's what she's doing in our office and she's amazing," Vic praised. "I never dreamed bookings at The Haven could be so easy. My phone is now linked with our system. It doesn't matter if I'm out, I can still see our openings at a glance. You have a gift, Liv, one God blessed you with abundantly. I wish He'd given me just a little of it."

"He blessed you with other things," Olivia said with a quick glance at Victoria's husband and daughter.

"Yes, He has. Is that everything on your list, Olivia?" Ben asked.

Gabe noticed Olivia's face redden before she ducked her head to consult her notes once again.

"There's more," he guessed with a wry smile.

"I do have a few other suggestions," Olivia admitted, looking embarrassed.

"Such as?" Gabe couldn't stop gazing at her, admiring the glistening fall of her dark hair against her newly sun-kissed cheek. "Hit us with them, Olivia."

"It's just—I wondered if it would be possible to get some roses planted at the corner of the deck. Art said Mavis used to have some there and she loved them, but what hasn't been winter-killed has been eaten by deer." She tugged out a small sheet of paper and laid it on the table. "Maybe something like this? Eli drew it for me."

"Eli drew this?" Gabe stared at the perfectly shaped rosebuds on a rosebush and the scattered shorter flowers beneath the bush that hugged the deck post. An almost invisible fence protected the flowers and, of course, birds fluttered nearby.

Gabe knew zip about art, but he recognized that his son was talented. How was he supposed to nurture that here, far away from teachers and special schools that knew how to encourage artistic stuff? Had Eve done anything about Eli's talent?

This fatherhood thing—he'd ask Olivia's advice. Again.

"We know the very person to create a lovely garden." Tillie studied the paper. "May we take this, Liv?"

"If Eli agrees," Olivia said, and asked the little boy.

"It's okay. I can draw more," Eli said. "I like drawin'. 'Specially birds."

"Thank you, dear. Our Jake is the most wonderful handyman we could ask for, but he's an absolute master at gardening. His specialty is roses. This would be the perfect project for him to show off his gift." Margaret leaned closer, peering through her bifocals. "You're very talented, Eli."

Eli shrugged and went back to playing.

"When the house gets painted, it might be nice to give the outbuildings a coat, also," Olivia murmured. "That way when they arrive home—Art said perhaps in two weeks—everything will look fresh and welcoming."

"We have a credit with the local painter. We'll ask him to paint the house," Aunt Tillie declared.

"Yes," Margaret agreed. "But I doubt our credit will cover more than the house."

"I'll paint the outbuildings," Gabe said, thrilled that his friends would be so well cared for.

"But you're already looking after Art's livestock. And you have Eli." Olivia frowned. "How are you going to have time for all this?"

Gabe didn't stop to think it over. He wasn't even sure where the idea came from. He only knew he liked it. A lot.

"Eli's going to help me," he announced. "We're going to paint those buildings together. Right, Eli?"

Eli blinked. He set down his game piece, thought for a moment then shrugged. "'Kay."

"Great." Olivia's smile was something to behold. It made her eyes sparkle. She glowed so much Gabe couldn't stop gawking at her. "Then the only thing left on my list is to find you and Eli a home."

"We need to pray on that," Tillie said firmly.

"Yes. God has a plan. That's why he sent Olivia and Eli to us." Margaret folded her hands. "Now we must discover that plan. Let's pray."

Gabe closed his eyes, but truthfully he didn't hear much of the aunties' prayers. He was too busy thinking about how Olivia fit in so perfectly with The Haven's ministries. Victoria certainly seemed delighted with her help, and in one afternoon she'd set things in motion that he'd struggled with for months.

How sad that she'd be leaving soon.

"How goes the search for a home for Eli and Gabe?" Victoria asked the following Thursday as she strolled into the office. She stopped, gulped. "What a mess!"

"The house search does not go well," Olivia said from her sitting position on the floor. "This mess is your old system of filing bills. But by tomorrow you'll be doing things differently and much more neatly."

"Okay." Victoria crunched on her apple as she watched her sister sift through the mass of files. "Did you take a call from social services about a weekend in July?"

"Yes."

"And they booked it?" Victoria asked, frowning when Olivia didn't immediately answer. "Liv?"

"I talked them out of it."

"You did what? Why?" Victoria's easygoing manner disappeared. "Olivia, the whole summer schedule revolves around—"

"That's the problem. It shouldn't." Olivia exhaled and rose, ready to calm her frustrated foster sister.

"But we—Olivia!" Vic exploded, staring across the office. "My wall. My charts. Everything's gone. What are you doing?"

"Making it better. I took your stuff down and painted this wall with chalkboard paint. When it's fully dry I'm going to draw a year's worth of calendars and mark in the bookings. Here's an idea of what it'll look like." She tapped the computer and a calendar appeared.

Victoria looked, frowned, but said nothing.

"See how you were always losing Friday night between groups? But everybody wants that night to start the weekend, right?" Olivia was so excited she barely waited for her Victoria's nod. "If we check out one group Friday morning and check in the next one that afternoon, the cabins don't stay idle overnight. You can accommodate more kids."

"But then I won't get a break and we'll have even less time to clean the cabins." Victoria's frustration was evident in her tone. "I need those few hours off, Liv, to spend with my kids and my husband."

"You need more than a few hours per week. That's why I've fitted in full days off for you." Olivia showed her the days marked in pink. "And you won't be cleaning the cabins, Vic."

"I won't?"

"Uh-uh. Each camping group and counselor will be responsible to clean their own cabin." Delighted with her plan, Olivia explained, "We'll have a contest and award prizes so they'll be eager to do a good job. One of your staff can do the final checkout."

"But who will handle the guests when I'm off?" Victoria's tone grew thoughtful.

"Again—your staff. They should all know how to deal with stuff like that anyway. You're the director, Vic, not the do-it-all girl." She grinned. "Another thing. We're going to change up the schedule so that everybody gets an occasional weekend off."

"Then we'll have to hire, train and house even more staff." Vic sighed. "Livvie, I know you mean well, but this is going to be expensive and cause so much more work for me—"

"No, it's going to streamline things so that you don't have to work so hard. Trust me, Vic. This will work." Olivia tamped down her frustration at her sister's dubious expression. Didn't Victoria realize that she knew what she was doing, that she'd handled far bigger and more complex scheduling issues than this? "I need you to call a staff meeting for this afternoon so I can explain how things are going to change. Is two o'clock okay?"

"Yes. But if this doesn't work, it's on you, Liv," Victoria warned. "You'll have to stay and pitch in. I can't take on any more."

"I know that. You're doing too much now, and you're worn-out. My schedule will fix that," Olivia reassured her gently. "Isn't that why you asked for my help? Please, trust me."

"I'll try." Clearly still troubled, Vic left.

Trust me. Such an easy thing to ask for, Olivia

thought. She used the words over and over each night at Eli's bedtime, trying to encourage him to talk about his past. But the child had yet to divulge details. His words from that first day still troubled her.

I prayed and prayed and he never came.

Why had Eli been praying for his father to come for him? What had his life with his mom, his aunt and her children been like?

Those questions whirled around without answers until Olivia finally forced them from her mind. She finished entering everything on the chalkboard, then checked and double-checked her work before deciding to take a break. It was lunchtime and she was starving. She strolled to the patio where Adele was busy grilling a picnic lunch. Olivia's stupid heart rate sped up to double time when Gabe sauntered up.

"Hi, there." He threw her that lazy-cowboy, knee-knocking smile of his and reached up to rub something from her scarred cheek.

Olivia jerked away, shifting her head so her hair covered the scar.

"Sorry. You had some blue chalk there." His smile didn't alter, which allowed her to relax a little. "Are you able to go house hunting this afternoon? I have a lead—"

"Victoria and I have a staff meeting at two o'clock," Olivia explained. "It should take about half an hour." Funny how much she wanted to go with him to look for a house. Why did it matter to her where Gabe lived?

For Eli's sake, she told herself. Her brain scoffed. *Eli. Right.*

"Meaning you'll be free after two thirty?" Gabe smiled at her nod. "Good." He stood there, studying her.

"What?" she demanded, suddenly uncomfortable.

"You know you want to ask," Gabe shot back with a smirk.

"Oh, brother." Olivia rolled her eyes. "Okay, the aunts say everything else is progressing well, so how's Eli doing with his painting on Art's outbuildings?" Truthfully? She was very curious, especially now because Gabe had insisted she see nothing until they were finished the entire job.

"Doing well." He burst out laughing at her disgust. "Patience isn't your strong suit, is it, Olivia?"

"Usually I'm a very patient person," she insisted. "You have to be when you work with logistics. It must be your effect on me."

"Sure," Gabe said.

Ignoring his amused chuckle, Olivia turned her back and sauntered toward the picnic table to fetch herself a hamburger. It didn't seem as if Adele had an overabundance of cooked burgers ready for the growing crowd of kids. She'd just selected a charred burger, intending to eat only the center when a long arm reached around her and replaced her meat patty with a less burnt one.

"What are you doing?" she demanded, whirling to glare at Gabe. "I like well-done burgers."

"That one passed well-done and moved into the 'ash' category a while ago. It's inedible." His grin somehow made her day brighter. "Mustard?"

"No, thanks. I prefer relish on my burgers." She moved her plate when he offered a scoop of raw onions. "No, thank you."

"Your loss." Gabe selected a serving of every single condiment offered, added a bag of chips and a glass of lemonade before following her to a grassy spot in the shade under a tree where Eli was eating with Mikey.

"Olivia, did anyone ever tell you you're not very adventurous?" Gabe asked in a mocking tone.

"No," she assured him, hiding her smile when he bit into one of the hot peppers her sister always served.

Gabe's eyes stretched wide. He stopped chewing, gulped, then grabbed his drink and downed the entire contents.

"Mostly people compliment me on avoiding the pitfalls of taking chances," she said smugly before holding out her own untouched glass. "Go ahead."

Gabe didn't refuse, simply took her glass and emptied it. She calmly ate her hamburger while he regained his breath. Then he carefully set aside the rest of the pepper. Finally, voice hoarse, he spoke.

"I still say you miss out on all the fun parts."

"Like you just did?" Olivia giggled. "Some things are missable, Gabe. Like Adele's ultrahot peppers. Is your painting going well, Eli?"

The child managed to utter about three words before Gabe reminded him that the painting was supposed to be a surprise. Eli shrugged at Olivia before returning to his lunch and Mikey's explanation about monster trucks.

"Good try," Gabe murmured. "Plying innocent kids with questions isn't very nice."

"Why is it such a secret? It's just an outbuilding." Frustrated by his refusal to tell her anything, Olivia huffed a sigh and concentrated on her lunch.

"Your strong suit is patience, huh?" Gabe laughed, then finished his hamburger. "Can I ask you a question?"

"Plying me with questions isn't nice, either," she shot back, surprised to find she enjoyed verbally sparring with him. "But you will anyway."

"Why don't you like to try new things?" Gabe set aside his empty plate and leaned back on his elbows.

"I am trying new things. I'm starting a new job in a new city, finding a new home and learning new skills. You're the one stuck in a bunkhouse, remember?" She shouldn't have said that, but Olivia knew exactly where his questions were leading. And she didn't like it.

"You've helped a lot with the program here. Don't you want to stay at The Haven and be part of the foster kids' ministry?" Gabe pressed curiously.

"I don't belong here. I'm only staying long enough to streamline things for Vic. When I'm finished, I'll go." She crunched on her chips as she surveyed the groups of kids chattering around them. "I'm not good with children, Gabe."

"Not true," he asserted. "You're very good with Eli." They watched as Eli and Mikey ran off.

"Not really. Eli's mostly self-sufficient. He doesn't tell me much. When we're alone together he doesn't talk about whatever's bothering him, and though I've tried, I haven't been able to elicit any information about his former circumstances."

"Me, neither," Gabe said glumly.

"You will." Olivia shrugged. "But kids and I just don't mesh. Never have."

"I think you could, but you won't let yourself unbend enough to get close to them." Gabe's blue eyes narrowed as he studied her. "I can't help wonder why that is when you're so competent at everything else."

"You know I'm competent how? Because you've seen

my fabulous sewing and cooking skills? As if!" She hooted with laughter, hoping to divert him. "You don't know that much about me, Gabe."

"I know some," he defended. "Your aunts told me you took a nothing job in the military and turned it into an example for other administrative assistants. I know the colonel you worked for was so impressed with your work that he signed off on you taking a bunch of courses that others were not offered. I know you were awarded several service honors and that you set up two other offices—"

"Enough. Let's agree that the aunts told you some stuff about what I do. Did." Olivia looked directly into his eyes. "Now add this to your knowledge. I freeze up around kids. I do stupid things and sometimes they get hurt. I'm lousy with responsibility for children so I avoid them. That way they don't get hurt." Irritated, she glared at him. "Can we drop it now?"

"For now." He grinned. "What kind of houses do you think we'll find this time?"

"I already know." She smiled triumphantly. "I've done some research."

"Ah, so you were intending to go house hunting with me again." He looked a little too pleased with himself.

"I was hoping you'd locate something you'd consider buying so Eli could have a home," she corrected. There was something about this cowboy with his pretense of slow-wittedness that annoyed Olivia no end because she knew Gabe was smart as a whip. "As I've said before, that kid needs his own home. And I need to get to work if I'm going to be able to leave with you after the meeting. Excuse me."

She rose and walked toward The Haven, fully aware

that Gabe's blue eyes followed her and eager to escape that pensive stare. But the aunties stopped her before she could enter the office.

"Livvie, dear, we fear we may have bragged on you a little too much with Gabe," Tillie said, looping her arm through Olivia's.

"It's just that we're so proud of you. But, well…" Margaret's voice dropped away.

"We know you like your privacy," Tillie finished.

"Yes, I did prefer that when I was with the military. And Gabe's just informed me of all the details you shared." She smiled at their worried looks. "Don't worry, Aunties. It's fine. But, please, don't tell him anything more, okay?"

"Why not?" Margaret frowned. "If he already knows most—"

"A girl should have some secrets." The moment she said it, Olivia wished she hadn't. Her aunts glanced at each other, speculative looks filling their faces. Looks Olivia knew too well. "Not that it matters one little bit," she quickly backtracked. "There is no relationship between us. I don't know Gabe very well and—"

"Not to worry, dearie. You'll get to know him a lot better now that you're home. Meantime, your secrets are safe with us." Tillie made a zipping-the-lip motion and winked.

"So, you're going house shopping—with this man you hardly know? How exciting." Margaret chuckled aloud as Olivia rolled her eyes. "We do love having you girls back with us at The Haven. It's such fun."

"I'm only home for a short while, remember. I can't stay." Given her aunts' glazed expressions, Olivia could only hope her cautioning words sank in.

"We know that's what you *said*, dear. Later." Tillie looped her arm in Margaret's and the two strolled away, whispering and giggling like girls.

"Olivia, you need to learn to shut up," she scolded herself. To enforce the words, she closed the office door and forced herself to concentrate on finishing the schedule plan. She intended to hand it out at the meeting later.

But it wasn't that easy to muffle the giddiness that burbled inside when she thought about the upcoming house hunt with Gabe. He was going to be so surprised.

Something was up.

After a quick glance at Olivia's face, Gabe took the back road as directed. She looked smug, too satisfied with herself.

"This track leaves something to be desired," he muttered as his truck almost bottomed out on the ruts.

"Once you're living here I'm sure the county will maintain the road." Olivia pressed her lips together firmly, stifling her smile.

Definitely something up, Gabe decided.

"Turn left here."

He obediently turned, rounding a huge grove of massive spruce trees. His foot fell off the gas pedal.

"Isn't it gorgeous?" Olivia whispered. "Forty acres. On the crest of the hill, protected against the north winds, facing south so you get the best light—well?" She studied his face eagerly.

Gabe parked, got out of the truck and soaked in the view. Green rolling hills undulated all around, perfect for a few horses to graze in. Trees, deciduous and evergreen, lay scattered in bunches here and there, offering shade. A small river dissected the land on the lowest level. Outcroppings of granite rock someone had piled here and there added to the variety of the scene.

"Outbuildings?" he managed to croak, shocked that he hadn't known about this lovely piece of land. "House?"

"There's a barn there." She pointed.

The reserve in her voice made Gabe study Olivia's face.

"Needs work," he grunted after a quick appraising glance. "And the house—" Words failed him at the sight of a burned-out black skeleton of what might once have been a two-story home. "Talk about a fixer-upper." Gabe frowned at her. "You were the one who said I need time with Eli. If I bought this place I'd spend ages building a house and we couldn't live here in the meantime, so—"

"That's the beauty of my plan." Olivia looked anything but defeated. "You don't have to."

"Good thing Eli didn't come," Gabe muttered, squinting at the charred ruins. "The kid would be terrified imagining living in that horror house. So am I."

"It's a teardown for sure." Olivia grinned as if that was perfect. "Come on. Let's take a closer look and I'll explain."

"This had better be good," he warned, slightly annoyed that they'd wasted time driving here.

"Oh, Gabe, it's very good." She stood in the sunshine, eyes sparkling, trim and neat in her jeans and red cotton shirt, looking as if she belonged on this land. "Look around. The ranch part is perfect, right?"

"Yes, but—"

"Great, we agree on the land. And the price?" She named a figure that made him blink.

"That can't be—"

"It's correct." She grinned, obviously delighted with her find. And why not? The setting was gorgeous.

"Great. Except for the house," he muttered.

"True. But what if you moved in a house, one that's mostly completed?" The silver sparkle in Olivia's gray eyes transmitted her enthusiasm. "A ready-to-move house."

"An RTM?" Gabe struggled to visualize it.

"It wouldn't be hard to move one onto the foundation once that road was taken care of." She held up a hand, forestalling his next comment. "RTMs aren't prohibitive costwise and they're well built. In fact, I got the idea from the aunts when they mentioned a man in the congregation who builds them. Apparently, he's trying to cut down on his stock to get some cash flow. Here, look at these."

Gabe stepped forward to look at the tablet she'd lifted from her purse.

"I chose two different styles that I thought might suit what Eli wants and what you need. Eighteen hundred square feet in the first house and twenty-five hundred in the second." She pointed out a variety of features in each, ending with, "Both have a big wall of windows that would overlook the valley and that magnificent view."

The cost was printed beneath each house.

"Affordable, right?" Olivia shrugged at his raised eyebrows.

"How—?"

"I did some research." She grinned. "It's what I do."

"Very well done, too." Gabe couldn't believe she'd gone to all this trouble for him. And Eli.

"The price may be negotiable if inventory is high," she suggested as if she knew his focus was on the price and whether he could swing it.

In the end, Gabe didn't get fixated on the money side of it. He grew entranced by the acres of land, virtually isolated, with not one single neighbor in view. In his brain a dream was forming of what he could create here, with Eli.

"Is this anything like what you wanted, Gabe?" Olivia murmured.

"Yes." Except that he hadn't known he wanted it so badly, hadn't known he'd ever be able to find something as special as this property. He faced Olivia. "Thank you," he murmured.

"You'll buy it?" she asked eagerly.

"I don't know. It's something to think about." Gabe watched her excitement fade. "What's wrong?"

"A beautiful piece of land like this isn't going to last," she said quietly. "Once it goes on the market, it will be snapped up in a minute."

"How did *you* find out about it?" he asked curiously.

"The aunts. They'd been visiting the fellow who owned this place. He moved into the nursing home in Chokecherry Hollow after the fire ruined his house. That's why the remains of the building haven't been cleaned up." As Olivia gazed into the valley, the sun highlighted her face. "He passed away last week. Tillie and Margaret talked to his only son, Edward, at the funeral. They learned he wants his father's estate settled immediately. Edward lives in Australia. He wants to get home to his family and his business. This is his phone number." She handed him a card with a number printed neatly on it. "I'm guessing this place will be listed before the end of the week. If you want it, you need to call immediately, Gabe."

"I have to think about it," he protested. "I can't just buy this place on the spur of the moment."

"Why not, if it's what you want and you feel it's a good price?" She gazed at him, utterly unaware that the wind had mussed her hair and left her scar revealed.

Not that it mattered to Gabe. He thought Olivia one of the most beautiful women he'd ever seen, elegant, sophisticated, talented and very clever. What he didn't get was why she wasn't married, or at least engaged. She must have had plenty of chances while working with the military.

"Gabe?" Her soft voice broke through his musings.

"I understand what you're saying." He struggled to gather his thoughts. "I'm still going to need a bit of time to think this over, check into some details."

"Of course," she agreed, walking back toward the truck with him. "But, Gabe?"

"Yeah?" He had to tamp down his reaction to the intensity of her expression as she studied him.

"Don't wait too long. Eli needs a home. So do you." She walked away.

Olivia thought he was needy? Or indecisive? He didn't like that. Not at all.

Gabe double stepped until he caught up to her at the truck.

"Have you got a few extra minutes?" he asked as they drove away.

"To do what?"

"Might as well take a look at those houses." He shrugged. "We'll detour through town on the way back to The Haven."

"Now you're talking," Olivia cheered. "Onward to the RTM builder."

"I wonder what Eli would think of the place," he mused.

"There's certainly a lot of grass." She winked at him, ticking it off on her slim fingers. "No neighbors to yell. He'd be able to have his tree wherever he wanted it. And he could even raise canaries if you made him a cage."

Gabe figured her delight was worth the effort of quashing his inhibitions about moving forward so fast.

Who knew organizing, scheduling, bossy Olivia would be the one to help him make a home for his son?

For the first time in years, Gabe was anticipating the future.

Chapter Four

Oblivious to the beauty from her favorite perch over-looking the gorgeous valley spread below her, Olivia tapped her phone several times, trying to make it come on. Finally the calendar flashed on screen. She stared at it in disbelief.

That couldn't be right. She'd now been at The Haven almost two weeks? That was well past her self-imposed deadline.

She studied the snowcapped mountains to her left. The days had flown past in a rush of activities and she'd loved every minute of being here. But she was getting too involved, and not just with The Haven's outreach to foster kids. Her heart ached for the quiet, solemn little boy who'd shown up the same day she had.

"Why the frown?" a voice behind her asked. "Phone out again?"

"For such a tall man, it's amazing how you creep up on people, Gabe," she snapped, startled by his sudden appearance.

"I *do not* creep." The cowboy's blue gaze narrowed. "I don't think I've ever heard you cranky, Olivia. Something must be wrong." He sank onto the grassy knoll beside her and, after a quick study of her face, turned his gaze on the lushly forested valley below them. "Want to share?"

"No. Thanks." She turned the question on him, so she wouldn't have to explain her sudden inexplicable yen to stay here. "Did you buy that land yet?" One look at his face said everything. "Gabe! It'll probably be listed soon, if it isn't already." Understanding dawned. "You couldn't get funding," she murmured sadly.

"The money's in place." He stretched out, legs in front, leaning back on his elbows to support his upper body. He looked completely relaxed. "That's not the issue."

"Then what is? Won't Edward sell it to you?" Reasons for his failure to act multiplied in her head. "Has he changed his mind about selling?"

"Nothing like that." Gabe's slow drawl, something Olivia usually enjoyed, suddenly irritated her.

"Then why in the world haven't you bought it?" she demanded.

"Because I'm not sure that's the right thing for Eli."

Gabe's soft-voiced response killed her irritation. This man was acting like a responsible father, putting his son's welfare first. How could she fault that?

"What specifically are you worried about?" she asked quietly.

"I work long hours at the Double M, Olivia. That won't change if I intend to keep my job, and I do." Gabe's pensive tone told her he'd given a lot of thought to this change. "I'd probably have to hire a housekeeper to maintain the house anyway, but I'd also want whoever that is to watch Eli until I get home. It's a lot of time for a kid to be alone."

"Or he could take the after-school bus with Adele and Vic's kids here to The Haven," Olivia mused aloud. "My sisters hired an after-school sitter who watches over the kids and plays with them until five or so. Maybe you could chip in for her pay and Eli could wait here for you to finish work," she proposed.

"It's an idea." He thought about it for a few minutes. "Probably better than him being at our home, or what could be our home."

"What makes you say that?" She couldn't understand the comment.

"Olivia, Eli has never lived in such an isolated place."

"But he said he wanted no neighbors," she protested, thinking she should have put more research into after-school care for kids, though she'd been very busy reorganizing the office and the schedule and a myriad of other details that had cropped up. "He wanted grass," she remembered.

"Eli can have all the grass he wants." Gabe laughed, then quickly sobered. "The rest—I'm not so sure. In theory, having no neighbors sounds great. Until you're alone and the coyotes are howling, or a blizzard is blowing in." Gabe shook his head. "Scary, especially if you're a little kid."

"You've really considered the angles," she said, unable to mask her admiration. "Good for you, Dad."

A tinge of red colored Gabe's jutting cheekbones before he tilted his Stetson down, which meant she couldn't read his expression.

"It's my job. I'm responsible for Eli now. I'm all he has. I want him to have a home, but most of all, I want him to be happy." His voice changed, grew sadder. "I don't think the kid had much of a life before Eve got sick, let alone after. I'm only guessing that since Eli hardly says a word, but a couple of his comments make me think somebody bullied him."

"I've wondered that, too." Olivia reached out and squeezed his hand in commiseration. "But that's the past. He's here now, Gabe, and you're not going to let that happen again. Eli's going to be very happy here. Especially when you get into your new home. *If* you get into it," she added with emphasis.

"Maybe." His dithering drove her crazy.

"You've come to The Haven every night to have dinner with him, to read him a bedtime story and say goodnight. That's all good," she said, nodding. "But it doesn't make The Haven Eli's home."

"No, it doesn't. And it doesn't make me his father, either. That's clear because he always asks you to listen to his prayers, even though I'm sitting right beside him." Gabe's face was a picture of hurt and confusion. "That's another reason I'm hesitating. I'm hoping that with a little time he'll get more used to me."

"Or maybe he'll get so used to staying at The Haven that it will become his home, instead of one you both live in together—eventually. Time will only make it harder when you move him." Olivia shook her head. "I doubt that's what you want, Gabe."

"What I want is for Eli to be happy." The low-voiced comment made her pay attention. "Even if it isn't with me," he added.

Mentally, Olivia cheered that Gabe was willing to deny himself for his son. He was going to be a great dad. But she also wanted him to be practical.

"That is all very selfless, until you remember the day Kathy dropped him off." Olivia couldn't explain why she felt compelled to help father and son bond. She only knew they couldn't—wouldn't—do that when they were mostly apart. "Eli said he *prayed* you'd come, Gabe," she reminded softly. "That doesn't sound like he doesn't want his dad. The two of you just need your own place and time alone together to figure out how to mesh."

"You make it sound like a marriage," he grumbled. "Bad comparison."

"Not all marriages are bad, Gabe." Olivia giggled at his glower.

"I've been told," he shot back, face grim. "But mine was bad enough that I'm not going to repeat the experience."

"I feel the same about marriage myself, though I never actually made it to the altar," Olivia agreed, then wished that hadn't slipped out.

Gabe sat up. "Why didn't you? Make it there, I mean?"

There it was, the question she'd been avoiding. She unclenched her jaw.

"Because I could never marry a liar."

"What did he lie about?" Brows pleating, the cowboy dad studied her.

"Everything. His love, me being beautiful, a future together. Most importantly about already being married. That kind of turned me off matrimony." She met his gaze and shrugged. "Doesn't matter now. It's over, finished, in the past. I do *not* want to talk about him or remember my stupidity in being so gullible that I believed every lie he spoke."

"I don't think it was a lie to say you're beautiful,

Olivia." Gabe's soft voice and gentle smile reached inside her and warmed a cold, hard place, but his words made her furious.

"You think this is beautiful," she demanded, pushing her hair off her cheek so her scar was on full display.

"It's a scar, sure." Gabe didn't flinch or turn away. In fact, he looked totally blasé. "I've got a few of my own. That's the cost of living. Visible or not, Olivia, everyone has scars."

"The point is, it's not beautiful," she muttered, half to herself. "And Martin didn't love me. He couldn't have."

"Why not?" Gabe was not going to let this go. She wished she'd never brought up the subject. "Olivia?" he pressed when she didn't answer.

"Because he was already married," she blurted. "He has two children. Can you believe I didn't know that, didn't guess?" Disgusted with herself, she tightened her arms around her knees. "Olivia, the great organizational expert, didn't have a clue she was being duped until her boss told her the ugly truth."

"Was Martin unhappy at home or something?" Gabe asked.

"Who cares? He was still living there, *with his wife and family.*" She blinked fast and furiously to suppress the tears. "Anyway, it didn't matter."

"Why not?"

"Because even if he'd got a divorce, I wouldn't have anything to do with him. I never want to be the cause of a family breakup. Besides that, I would never be first in his life. I don't want to be someone's second best." She glared at him. "Don't you dare say a word about this to anyone, Gabe Webber. It's not for public consumption."

"Of course not." His moue of disdain somehow made

her feel better. "What a pair we are with our terrible taste in the romance department."

They were a pair?

"Back to the point," Olivia said after a moment, uncomfortable with the picture his words drew in her brain. "I still believe you and Eli need to get into your own place as soon as possible."

She hesitated, wanting to say more. But to do so meant she'd risk offending Gabe. And yet, maybe it was worth it if it would get this cowboy and his son to begin bonding.

"You know, it's none of my business, but I was thinking. Maybe part of what went wrong between you and Eve," she began tentatively, not liking the way his whole face tightened, "was not being alone together. Maybe if there'd been just the two of you, you'd have been forced to work things out."

"You're wrong," Gabe said flatly. "Lack of togetherness isn't what went wrong with my marriage. Our failure wasn't due to my father's presence. He never interfered. In fact, he made it a point to be away most evenings. Actually, so did Eve." His face tightened; his lips pinched together. "I told you—all she wanted was good times and money. Period."

Olivia sighed. Gabe sounded so bitter, so hostile when he spoke about Eve. That couldn't help with his attempts to bond with Eli.

"Are you thinking it was a hardship for Eve to live on our ranch?" he snarled a moment later. "It wasn't. My father did very well. We had a huge house, several vehicles, everything we needed."

She waited, somehow knowing he wanted to vent.

"Married to me, Eve had a respected name in the

community, a nice home, somebody who loved her like a fool," he added, blue eyes blazing. "She threw it away for money, money my dad gave her, so I could be free of her. It was my fault he died. I married her against his wishes and he paid for it."

"Oh, Gabe." Olivia's heart ached for the young man who'd been so disillusioned by love and was still hurting. Not that she'd done much better. But at least she'd been able to write off Martin's pretense of loving her and move on to embrace a new life.

Have you really?

"I do not want to talk about Eve." Cold and hard, the words seemed dragged from him.

"Me, neither. Let's talk about Eli." Olivia squared her shoulders and faced facts, as she always did when dealing with a problem. "Have you watched him with the other kids? He never just grabs a toy and joins in with them. He always waits until all the toys have been chosen, and then he picks up one and tries to amuse himself with it."

"So?" Gabe arched an eyebrow.

Lord, help me say this so it helps him. Olivia inhaled and let the words flow.

"So, I know exactly what that's like. Every single foster home I was ever in gave me the same feeling," she said as grim memories assailed her. "It wasn't always that someone was mean to me or wouldn't let me use the toys. It was mostly that I didn't feel like anything was mine, that I had a right to play with their stuff."

"Why did you feel like that?"

"I guess because it wasn't my home and they weren't my things. Because no matter what anyone told me, I knew I didn't belong there." She paused. "I wonder if Eli feels the same?"

"He'll get over that once he gets used to everyone here," Gabe said with a shrug.

"Not necessarily."

"Why not?"

To explain she had to tell him a little more about her past.

"I didn't. I went through the motions of living here at The Haven, but it wasn't my home. My foster aunties tried to help me understand that no one was going to come and take me away. That I could stay here, that I could let myself love them and my sisters." Frustrated that Gabe hadn't seemed to notice his son's aloof behavior, Olivia struggled to gain his understanding. "Aunt Tillie and Aunt Margaret kept at it, and I did finally relax, but sometimes I still don't feel like I belong here, that The Haven is my home."

"You're saying Eli needs ownership of where he lives."

"Yes." She exhaled. "Once he's at home, other kids can come over and he can be the one to say, 'Play with anything you want. It's my stuff and I don't mind sharing.' That's when he'll gain confidence." Olivia hadn't thought about it for eons, but suddenly the feeling of not belonging anywhere returned full force. Where did she belong now?

"I'm not sure—" Gabe's nose wrinkled, showing his disbelief.

"I was left at a hospital as a baby. I never knew my parents, never knew where I came from or where I'd be sent next. It's a horrible feeling for a kid, Gabe. In a way, Eli's going through the same thing. His mom's gone. His aunt dumped him off. You leave him at The Haven. He doesn't know what to expect next. He needs control and stability in his world. He needs a home to come home to."

"I guess." Gabe studied her as if she were a total stranger. "I knew your aunts fostered you. I didn't know the rest."

"I don't like to talk about those days." Wasn't that the truth?

"I'm glad you told me. It helps me understand some of Eli's issues." His gentle smile made her feel better about blabbing her life's history.

"That land is what you want, Gabe. You said so. If you and Eli choose the house together, it would make it seem more like you're a family and that you value his opinion, that he has some say in what's happening to him. It will give him ownership in the place he'll eventually call home."

"I guess you're right."

"Good." She exhaled, then blurted out the next part. "But you have to act. You can't keep waiting for the perfect situation to happen along because it won't. And you'll have lost this opportunity."

"Okay, okay. I get it, Olivia." Gabe straightened from his lounging position and held up his hands in surrender. "I'll call the guy and make an offer."

"Now?" she pressed, afraid he'd come up with more excuses once he left.

"Can we say pushy?" He rolled his eyes at her before pulling out his phone. Then he frowned. "I don't have the number with me."

"I memorized it." Olivia recited the numbers, thrilled that Gabe was finally doing this.

"I should have known you would, Ms. Organizer," he muttered, flicking the phone on to speaker. When it was answered, he gave his name and said he was interested in purchasing the land.

Olivia sat, elbows on her knees as she listened to the back-and-forth discussion, trying to stem her excitement when they agreed on a price and a possession date.

"I'm really happy to see Dad's land go to someone with family," the seller, Edward, told Gabe. "I have so many wonderful memories of times there, with my dad. My mom left us when I was little, so the two of us were on our own. But Dad made the place a wonderful home for a kid. It's good to hear you intend to do the same with your son, Gabe."

After discussing details, Gabe finally hung up looking bemused.

"Congratulations. You've taken the first step to making a home for Eli." Olivia tried to hide her delight, but judging by his expression, Gabe saw her satisfaction.

"You're the one who got me into this," he grumbled, tucking his phone into his pocket. "You better not leave until Eli and I are settled in that house."

"No guarantee of that. But I can probably stay another couple of weeks." *You weren't going to get involved, remember? Fresh start in Edmonton?* She shoved away the nagging voice in her head.

"Why are you grinning like that, Olivia?" Gabe grumbled.

"Because I just had a great idea. Let's go get Eli and show him where his home is going to be." She jumped up and held out her hand. "Come on, Gabe. Smile. This is a happy day."

He did grasp her hand, but it wasn't for help to get

up. He rose on his own, his fingers tightening around hers as he studied her face.

"If this doesn't work out," he began, but she wouldn't allow it.

"Enough with the naysaying," she ordered, and yanked her hand from his. She had to, in order to stop the electric current shooting up her arm. "This is going to be the best decision of your entire life, cowboy."

The best decision of his life?

Gabe wasn't so sure when he saw Eli's lack of response to the land he'd just purchased.

"Can you just imagine it, Eli?" A very excited Olivia pointed out features. "Your dad could hang a tire swing from that tree. And you could make a hideaway place in the caragana hedge over there. I used to do that."

Gabe grinned. The woman was like a kid herself as she outlined possibilities for what would be Eli's home.

"Do you think you'd be okay to live here?" Gabe finally interrupted, worried when Eli kept looking around without saying a word.

"It's very—big." Eli gulped.

"There's lots of grass," Gabe reminded. "You said you liked that."

"Yeah." Hesitant or afraid?

"We'd need a dog." Stark fear filled Eli's face at Gabe's comment. He immediately revised. "Maybe a puppy would be better. Where I work they have a dog who's going to have puppies soon."

"A little dog?" Eli asked timidly.

"The puppies would be small at first, but they'd grow. Just like you," Gabe added. Maybe this was all too much for the kid. Maybe he should have done some work on the place first.

"It can't hunt birds?" the boy insisted.

"We'll teach it not to." Was that his imagination or did Eli's shoulders relax a little?

"There's lot of trees." Eli wandered over to a row of poplar trees that lined the driveway. "Birds live here, right?" he asked Olivia.

Gabe's heart sank. *I'm right here, son. Talk to me.*

"I don't know much about birds, Eli." Olivia hunkered down to look into his eyes. "But your dad has lived around here for a long time. You should ask him."

Eli looked at Gabe soundlessly.

"Owls, chickadees, robins, swallows, geese on the pond, blue jays. Those are just a few of the birds that live in these parts." Gabe watched Eli digest that.

"Are chickadees like canaries?" His son's blue eyes sparked with interest.

"Not exactly. Sometimes they have a bit of yellow on their stomachs," Gabe explained. "But mostly they're kind of gray and brown so they can hide in the bush. Sometimes in the summer we get a bird that looks a lot like a canary, though I think they're a variety of finch. They usually come if you feed them niger seed, but they always leave for the winter."

"They gotta eat." Interest flared in Eli's eyes. "So I can draw 'em."

"Sure. We'll build a feeder. No problem." Gabe heaved a sigh of relief. One hurdle over.

"Then I think it'd be good," Eli said quietly. "'Cept I don't like that house."

"It will be gone. There will be a new one in its place,"

Gabe assured him. "But we'll have to pick it out before they can deliver it."

"Oh." Eli fell silent, apparently intrigued by a house moving.

"We'll have to leave pretty soon," Olivia said. "The party for Art and Mavis is supposed to start in an hour." She mussed Eli's hair with a smile. "I can hardly wait to see your painting."

"The secret will be over then." Eli looked at Gabe, his little face very serious. "It's okay?"

"It looks beautiful, son. You did an amazing job." Gabe's heart sang at this first bit of father-son sharing. "Before we leave, let's walk around where our house will go. You can tell me if you think we need to add some other things."

Eli turned to survey the road they'd driven in on, then looked at him with a question in his eyes. Gabe burst out laughing.

"I agree. Getting that road graded should be number one on our to-do list." He caught Olivia's glance on him. Her gray eyes shone approvingly, and that sent a ruffle of warmth shooting through him.

Surprised by this unusual reaction, Gabe asked himself why. Olivia was a friend, a good friend. He wasn't interested in anything more. Was he?

They spent the next half hour chatting about possibilities. Olivia had many suggestions, some outlandish, but most extremely practical. She was a natural at organization, at seeing possibilities. She was the one who'd encouraged him to take this step. Gabe needed to think of a way to thank her.

"We've got to get a move on if we're going to make it

to the housewarming," she chided him after he'd fallen into thought.

"Okay. Wait a minute." Gabe reached out and plucked a leaf from her hair, then brushed a ladybug off her shoulder. "Okay, good to go."

"Thanks." She seemed to suddenly withdraw though he was fairly certain she never moved a muscle.

"Olivia?" he asked, confused. "Is something wrong?"

"Of course not. Let's go." Whirling away, she raced Eli to his truck, helped the child into the middle and climbed in behind him. The slam of her door made Gabe stir. He gave her a quick glance after he'd started the truck, but Olivia was turned away, her face hidden.

It felt like something had changed between them.

But what?

Chapter Five

"Ta-da." Gabe ripped away the paper covering their artwork on the outbuilding.

"It's marvelous!"

As Olivia gushed over their painting at Art's ranch, Gabe stood with the paper balled in his arms, grinning like an idiot.

"Where did you learn how to do this?" she asked Eli. "Those baby birds in the nest and the little squirrel carrying an acorn—they're beautiful." As if aware she'd excluded him, she twisted to smile at Gabe. "Your painting is nice, too," she offered.

"Nice." He burst out laughing. "Timid praise indeed, Olivia." In the moment that his gaze held hers, he noticed she was blushing. She quickly turned away. "Eli and I make a good painting team."

"You sure do. In fact, this whole place looks amazing." She clasped her hands like a kid awaiting Christmas. Just another thing Gabe appreciated about Olivia. She wholeheartedly delighted in another's joy. "I can hardly wait for Art and Mavis to get here."

"Don't have to wait. Here they come," he said, just

loudly enough for the assembled group to hear. Everyone stilled, watching the elderly couple's car slow and then stop in the driveway. Eyes wide, Art took it all in before helping Mavis out of the car.

"Welcome home," Aunt Tillie said as she hurried forward to welcome the pair.

"We hope you won't mind that we took some liberties," Margaret added, matching her sister step for step.

"Some? You've done so much," Mavis breathed. "Roses! They're stunning. And the house." She took in each of the changes with little gasps of joy. "Look what they've done, Art," she crowed. "Just look."

"I see it, girl. New paint, new roof, deck's fixed—oh, it's too much." Tears welled and rolled down his weary face. "How can we ever thank you?"

"You don't thank friends for helping out, Arthur." Gabe stepped forward and shook his hand.

"He's right." Tillie smiled. "You're our friends. We love you. We don't want you moving away from us because of a few little problems."

"A few? Oh, my!" Mavis gaped at the outbuildings that Gabe and Eli had painted. "Who did that?"

Gabe watched as Olivia eased Eli forward and explained. Mavis wrapped her arms around the boy and hugged him fiercely.

"If you knew how often I've sat here, wishing for something prettier to look at. I just love those birds, Eli," she said softly. "Thank you."

"Welcome," Eli answered politely, looking, Gabe thought, a little shocked by all the attention.

Duty done, Gabe now encouraged his son to join the other kids, which Eli did, though he stood to one side until Mikey grabbed his hand.

"It's a glorious day, so come enjoy your deck, my dears," Margaret enthused. "The men built this ramp for you to get up and down more easily." She hooked her arm in Mavis's and, with Tillie on the other side, walked the woman slowly up the incline and escorted her to one of the big wooden chairs with their gaily striped cushions.

"Those cushions weren't here yesterday." Gabe glanced at Olivia, knowing they were another of her "ideas."

"I only finished them last night. Adirondack chairs are comfortable, but according to Aunt Margaret, a little padding doesn't hurt." She tilted her head to one side. "Are the fabrics too bright? I pieced from Aunt Tillie's quilt stash to make the cushions and the hanging."

"I think they look amazing." He studied the *Welcome* hanging for a minute. "You used the dark green of the trim—was that color your choice?"

"The painter asked the aunties. They asked me and, well—" She blushed but nodded. "I heard Mavis loves green. It seemed appropriate."

"I don't know how you do it." He stared at her. "I've known this couple for ages and I never knew about Mavis's preference for green. Yet you're here for a couple of weeks and..."

"Something the aunts mentioned." As usual Olivia shrugged off his praise though she looked pleased. "Aunt Tillie suggested using the same tone for a feature wall in the living room. I checked, and it looks stunning with that wood floor and the cream walls."

"The cream was also your choice. And perfect," Gabe added, seeing the truth on her face.

Everyone paused as the pastor asked a blessing over

their picnic. He then invited folks to savor the lemonade and fresh cherry pie.

"Adele?" Gabe guessed.

"She wanted to contribute. Since the cherries are early this year and very plentiful..." Olivia blushed again at his knowing look. "I thought it would be a shame not to take advantage of the bounty, that's all."

"That's all," he agreed with a grin.

"Want to get in line?" she asked, ducking her head in that way she had that hid her expressive eyes.

"Of course." He panned a droll look. "When have you known me to miss out on pie, Olivia?"

"Right, silly question." She glanced around. "I love the benches scattered here and there. One under that big maple, another beside the roses and a third near the garden. Who built them?"

"Ben conned me into helping him do it. *After* he saw a sketch *you* left lying around." Gabe's admiration for the way her brain brimmed with ideas had grown exponentially in the past weeks.

"Not much of a sketch compared to Eli's work," she demurred before speaking to a burly man in front of them. "Thanks for making those metal picnic tables, Victor. They're amazing."

"Welding part was easy," the man said with a grin. "The wife painted 'em with enough coats of weather-resistant paint they should be good outside for many years. I'm glad you thought of a way I could help. I can just see Art and Mavis feedin' their grandkids on 'em."

"Me, too," Olivia agreed with a—wistful?—smile. Something glinted in her eyes. Longing? For this? Well, no wonder. He thought a do like this was pretty special, too.

After they'd retrieved their pie, Gabe's coffee and her lemonade, they found a lush grassy spot under a flowering lilac and sat down together. He ate in contented silence, occasionally glancing around to greet friends and neighbors who'd come to welcome the couple home. For Gabe this was what life was about—communities caring for each other. He was thrilled his two friends would now find life much easier on their beloved ranch.

"Is there anything you don't think of, Olivia?" Gabe asked, noticing several burgeoning planters strategically placed here and there. That had happened sometime after his departure yesterday, too. Good thing he'd covered Eli's painting. "You have your fingers in a lot of lives around here. Chokecherry Hollow, The Haven, the church. Our whole community is better off for you being here, receiving your special touch."

"I haven't done much, but that's nice of you to say. You like it here a lot, don't you, Gabe?" Her silver-gray eyes studied him.

"I do. I chose Chokecherry Hollow because it's very much like the small community I grew up in. Neighbors caring for neighbors. Like today." Satisfaction bloomed inside at the sound of laughter and happiness filling the yard. How could Eve *not* have wanted this life?

The same old flare of antagonism threatened to spoil his afternoon, so Gabe tamped it down. Memories of Eve couldn't be allowed to tarnish one second of his time with Olivia.

"I've loved my holiday here." She looked around as if she was fixing the scene in her mind to take out and remember later. Her gaze lingered for a moment on Eli, who still hadn't joined in playing with the other kids. She moved as if she was about to go to him but then the dreamy expression in her eyes drained away. That fear of getting too close to children again, Gabe guessed.

"You love it here, but you'll still leave The Haven?" It wasn't really a question. He could see the resolve fill her face.

"Of course. I start a new job in September, remember?" Olivia calmly finished her lemonade.

"September?" Gabe frowned in confusion. "I had the impression it started next month."

"Nope. September 21," she said.

"But this is only June. What's the rush to leave? Summer is very busy at The Haven. They could use an extra pair of hands," he said with a frown. "Especially your organizing hands."

"I've already stayed longer than I intended to, Gabe. I need some time to organize my new life. I don't know Edmonton anymore after so many years living in the East. It will take time to find a place to live. Also, I'm not as familiar as I'd like to be with my new employer's business, so I need time to prepare with some research."

"You and your research." He caught her watching Eli's attempt to befriend a child afraid of Art's dog.

"Research is what I do, Gabe," Olivia said absently. A slight smile curved her lips. "Look at your son. He's making friends."

"That's also thanks to you," he said quietly. "You've helped Eli feel comfortable when I couldn't. I appreciate it. But there's so much more he needs to figure out and I'm not sure how to help him or what to do to get him to truly trust me."

"You *do* know, Gabe. It's all in here." She tapped his chest, right over his heart. "Just be his dad, day in, day out. Love him. No matter what. You'll figure it out." She shrugged as if it was simple. "Anyway, it's not like I'm leaving tonight. I have a few more days here."

"Good." He grinned. "In that case can you come with Eli and me to look at houses tomorrow?"

"What's the rush?" Olivia said, but he sensed her approval. "I had to nag you to buy that land. You were very reluctant."

"Now the decision's made I want to get on with creating a home for Eli." Gabe arched one eyebrow. "I think it would be good to get him settled before school starts. Don't you agree?"

"Wholeheartedly," she assured him with a smile.

Had she agreed only for Eli's sake? Or did she really believe in his ability to be a good dad?

They spent the next two hours visiting with others who'd stopped by to welcome Art and Mavis home. Then Olivia said she needed to get back to The Haven.

Gabe didn't want to hear that. He enjoyed her company and didn't want it to end. Not enjoyed her company in the romantic sense, he told himself, but because he had nowhere to go except back to his bunkhouse, where he'd be alone again since Eli was going to a new friend's house for something called a playdate, which Olivia had arranged.

Pathetic life, cowboy.

Nevertheless, he asked her, "What's the rush to leave?"

"I'm rebooting The Haven's entire computer system tonight so the new programming can take effect. That means going offline," she explained after they'd said goodbye and Gabe was driving toward The Haven. "Probably at midnight since Vic doesn't need anything then. But once it's back up and running, I have to go through everything, make sure there aren't any glitches before they start using it again."

"Sounds like a big deal," he mused, wishing he was more computer literate so he could understand exactly what Olivia was doing.

"It won't be a big deal if my new program runs as planned. If it doesn't—" She made a face. "Let's just say I intend to have everything running smoothly by the time The Haven wakes up tomorrow morning."

"Meaning you'll be up all night—again." Eli had told him how _he'd_ woken last night to see Olivia walking her Aunt Tillie up and down the hall to work off some type of severe leg cramp.

Gabe admired Olivia's stamina. She couldn't have had much rest last night. She'd had a full day with Victoria's office to-do list, and he was pretty sure she'd already made several trips to Art and Mavis's before he'd met up with her at noon yet still looked fresh and ready to take on more challenges.

"I'm a little nervous about the reboot. Pray that all goes well, will you, Gabe?" she said quietly as they pulled onto The Haven's circular driveway.

"Sure." He wondered about the uncertainty in her voice. "Do you pray about your work a lot?" he asked, then grimaced. "Sorry. Too personal."

"It's okay." Olivia shrugged. "I pray a lot about everything. I just don't feel like I get answers very often." She grimaced. "Don't tell my aunties that."

"I'm sure they've gone through the same thing," he said quietly, surprised Olivia had doubts about her faith. He'd never have imagined this competent woman doubted anything.

"Maybe when they first became missionaries they

had doubts, though I doubt it. I'm pretty sure the aunties' faith is rock solid now and has been for years." She tilted her head to one side. "What about you?"

"What about me?" Gabe didn't want to talk about himself when she watched him so closely.

"When you pray, do you feel like you get the answers you need, Gabe?"

He inhaled. It was an honest question. He couldn't just brush her off, but he didn't have a good answer, either.

"Sorry. Too personal." Olivia shook her head, her face rueful. "Never mind."

"I don't always feel like I get the answers I want," Gabe admitted quietly. He switched off the motor and silence yawned between them. Olivia had asked for his help and he wanted to give it, to give back something in return for all she'd done for him and Eli. "The pastor did a study on prayer a while ago," he mused aloud. "It really made me think about how I pray, not that I'm great at it, but it did bring a new perspective."

"Go on." Olivia studied him as if she needed to hear his answer.

"I don't know if I can recall everything he said." She waited, hands folded in her lap, so Gabe shrugged and repeated what he remembered. "Basically, he started with trust. If we trust God, really trust Him, we can live without worry because we'll expect He'll take care of us. The 'cast your cares' verse figured into that lesson a lot."

"Because?" Olivia's intense scrutiny made him want to get it right.

"Because true trust means we don't worry and fret." Gabe watched her frown. "It's not easy to trust, but I remind myself every day that God's in control, that growth takes time. If I'm still worried, then I tell Him that. That's when peace comes." *Usually.*

"Right away?" Olivia asked, eyes wide.

"Sometimes." Gabe shrugged.

"I've struggled with this for so long," she admitted, her voice tight. "I want to trust God, but nothing happens when I pray."

"Nothing happens immediately, you mean? Or you don't see anything happening?" Gabe cautioned himself to be careful. He was no spiritual leader, but the strain in her face made him want to share what he'd learned. "It's funny, but since Eli's appearance I think I understand certain aspects of God a bit more."

"Really?"

"It sounds weird." Gabe hesitated before deciding to just say it and let Olivia make of it what she would. "Those words of Eli's—that he'd prayed and prayed for me to come—they stick in my head. I got thinking about how I've prayed and prayed for something."

"And?" she nudged verbally, eyes wide.

"I think sometimes God doesn't answer right away because He's trying to stretch our faith." Though he felt silly trying to explain something he'd never articulated, Olivia seemed eager for him to continue. "It's not that He can't do whatever we ask. But it's like when you were a kid at Christmas and you so desperately wanted something—a doll, maybe?" He looked at her to see if that made sense.

"A laptop," she murmured.

"Of course." He made a face. "You dreamed and thought about and planned all the things you'd do with that laptop, right? And all the while you waited, expecting your aunts would put it under the tree for you because you knew they loved you and wanted you to be happy." He stopped, uncertain if this was a good comparison.

"They gave me a lovely silver one. I used it until I finished university," she told him.

"You trusted them with your desire because you knew they loved you, but you had to trust and believe and wait until Christmas." He sighed. "What I'm trying to say, badly, is that I think sometimes God makes us wait so we can really think about what we're asking for, because we often say, 'I want this, I want that,' but it's really only a momentary fleeting thing that we forget about in a few minutes, or as soon as the next thing strikes our fancy."

"I've done that." Olivia flushed as if embarrassed by the admission.

"Me, too." Gabe nodded, a little distracted by her sad expression. "So, if we believe God is good and just and faithful, then we can be confident and rest in the knowledge that He will answer our prayers—but in His own time. We don't have to worry and struggle over things we don't control. We can rest in God and let Him work it out."

She stared at him as if surprised.

Gabe gulped, felt his face burn. "I sound like some kind of preacher," he muttered.

"You sound very smart." She kept watching him.

"Why did you ask me about this, Olivia?" he asked after a few moments had passed. And then he knew. "It's this thing you have about kids getting hurt around you, isn't it?"

She nodded, tears welling and spilling over her cheeks.

"I love my nieces and nephews so much and I want

to be close to them, to have them hug me and be able to hug them back, to take them on walks and find special bugs or pretty stones or watch a doe and her fawn. But then I remember the past and fear takes over and I'm terrified I'll cause them harm." She looked at him, eyes huge and glossy in her lovely face. "What if God never answers my prayer to be free of that, Gabe? What if I'm always going to be afraid?"

Gabe didn't really understand all she was suffering, but he couldn't stand to watch Olivia weep, to see her quiet desperation. He slid his arm around her shoulders and drew her close, allowing her to cry out the worry and fear that dogged her while he silently prayed.

"I'm sorry." She sniffed as she drew away a few moments later. "I've soaked your shirt."

"Olivia, have you talked to anyone about this?" When she shook her head, he frowned. "You should at least talk to your aunts."

"I don't want them to see how spiritually weak I am," she whispered.

"You're not spiritually weak," he said firmly.

"Then—?" She frowned at him, raised her shoulders helplessly.

"I'm no psychologist but I think inside you're afraid that God won't give you what you want, that is, freedom from this fear you carry." Gabe wasn't sure where the knowledge came from. He only knew it seemed right. "I don't know much about your past, but I'm guessing you became an organizer because you felt you had to take care of yourself, because nobody else would."

"How did you know?" she gasped.

"I didn't, but—that's how Eve was." He did *not* want to talk about his ex-wife, but some distant memory flickered in the recesses of his mind. "Even though I loved her, when I think about it now I realize that no matter how many times I said it, she never really seemed to believe me. And the reason she didn't was because she didn't trust me." The burst of knowledge burned like fireworks in his brain.

"Does knowing that make it easier to forgive her?" Olivia murmured.

Gabe stared at her and in that instant the gut-burning fury flared again.

"No," he snapped.

"Sorry." Olivia drew away, opened the door and stepped out of his truck, her face thoughtful.

"Wait," Gabe chewed himself out for not wording that properly. "I was trying to say that God tells us He loves us, but if we don't believe it and trust in it, it doesn't do us any good."

"You're right. I need to think about that." She gave him a funny smile. "Thanks for sharing, Gabe. See you tomorrow—after lunch?"

He nodded, watching as she closed the truck door, walked to The Haven and disappeared inside. He drove to the Double M with the pastor's words from that study on prayer echoing inside his head.

You're afraid to trust God because you don't ask for His will to be done. You want Him to do your will. That never works. Trust only comes when we want God's will more than we want our own.

While you're thinking about that, consider this. Maybe your prayers aren't answered because God's waiting for you to take care of something that gnaws and festers inside you.

Obviously, God wanted Gabe to forgive Eve.

"I can't," he said bitterly as he shoved the gearshift into Park and climbed out of his truck. "I can't just forget everything she cost me. Dad. Our ranch. Love. Eli."

He'd forgotten that kids from The Haven were coming for an evening trail ride. They would end the event with a big campfire. Gabe changed clothes and then went to chop wood. Maybe if he wore himself out he wouldn't have to think about Eve and the past and everything he'd lost.

Maybe.

Two nights later, weary from the reboot but satisfied that The Haven's systems were working properly, Olivia perched on the edge of Eli's bed to finish his bedtime Bible story and wondered where Gabe was. She hadn't seen him last night. Was he upset with her? Was he angry at her for asking about forgiving Eve?

"David was brave, right, Livvie?" Eli watched her closely. "He wasn't scared of that big giant." His solemn face studied her. "Do you get really scared?"

"Yes." *I have my own giants.* Immediately her mind time traveled back to her childhood and the day of the fire. With those memories came the usual blanket of guilt. Why hadn't she searched just a minute longer? Tried a little harder?

"Why d'you get scared?" Eli wanted to know.

"Somebody got hurt because I couldn't help them," she said brusquely, not wanting to elaborate and leave him with bad thoughts before he went to sleep. Actually, she didn't want to remember at all. "I tried, but I was so scared I couldn't help. That's why they got hurt."

"Is that why my mom died? 'Cause I was scared?" His voice dropped. "I tried to be a good boy. I din't tell when Bobby pinched me real hard or when April hit-ted me with the belt 'cause Mommy said I had to be a good boy so she'd get better." Tears rolled down his cheeks. "But I musta not been good enough 'cause she didn't get better."

"No, Eli, that's not right." Olivia ached to wrap him in her arms and rock away his sadness and guilt, but she couldn't. Fear kept her frozen in place. Better not to build the bonds and make herself responsible. All she could do was try to dispel his sad thoughts with words. "You didn't do anything wrong, sweetheart."

"But you said—"

"It isn't the same." Olivia now wished she hadn't brought up the past. Going back only added to her culpability.

"Why?" Eli was obviously struggling to comprehend.

"Well." How was she supposed to word this so the kid wouldn't feel responsible for his mother's death? "Your mom needed to know you were okay with your aunt."

"How come?" He wrinkled his nose.

"Because if she knew you were okay, she wouldn't worry about you and that made her feel better. You kept her happy by not telling. The only thing is…" She paused, struggling to find the right words. "If someone is nasty like Bobby and April were, I think you needed to tell someone, Eli. You couldn't tell your mom, I know that. She was too sick." She rushed to reassure him, anxious to dispel his worry. "But if someone hits you or pinches you like that again, tell your dad or me or someone, okay?"

"But you're goin' away." His frown matched the sinking of her heart.

"Not forever and, anyway, your dad will be here.

He'll always protect you, no matter what." Of that at least Olivia had no doubt. "Promise that if anything bothers you or makes you uncomfortable, you'll tell your dad about it right away. Okay?"

"'Kay." Eli relaxed against the pillow, his face thoughtful. "Who'd you tell?"

"Pardon?" Olivia blinked, surprised by his question.

"When the person got hurted 'cause you din't help." He studied her unblinkingly. "Who'd you tell 'bout it?"

"Nobody," she whispered.

"But you said—"

"It's bedtime, sweetie." She pulled the covers up to his chin and smiled. "Want me to listen while you say your prayers?"

"Yes, please." Eli squeezed his eyes closed and began talking as if God was sitting right there beside her in the armchair.

Olivia marveled at the simplicity of his prayers, and the sincerity with which he thanked God for his new friends, The Haven, and, of course, the birds he was learning to identify. He stumbled a bit when he came to the end of his *God Blesses*, hesitating before he added Gabe to the long list. He did not say *Dad*. There was an uncertainty underlying his words that said he wasn't quite sure how to pray for the man now in his life.

That hesitation pained Olivia. Her arms ached to enfold the little boy, to hold him close and assure him that Gabe wouldn't allow anything bad to happen to him ever again. But nobody could guarantee that. More than anything she wanted to promise to be there if Eli needed her. But she couldn't say that, either, because she wouldn't be here. Her future didn't lie at The Haven, and, anyway, forming the bond between this child and his father was the most important thing.

Eli had just whispered, "Amen," when Gabe added his own "Amen" as he set his Stetson on the floor.

"I'm sorry I'm so late, Eli," he apologized. "Some cattle broke through a fence and I had to round them up."

Olivia moved so Gabe could kneel at the side of Eli's bed. He, at least, had no hesitation about touching his son, his hand smoothing unruly strands so like his own, his smile lifting the corners of his lips.

"That was a good prayer," he said softly. "I think God likes it when we thank Him for all the things He gives us."

Eli watched him.

Gabe finally kissed the top of his head, murmured a good-night, then rose and switched off the main light, leaving a tiny night-light burning. Olivia preceded him out of the room and waited until he'd closed the door before walking down the stairs.

"I'm sorry I had to cancel our house hunt. It's been crazy busy, and now I've got to get back to the Double M," he said apologetically. "We have a couple of sick horses. Can I let you know about looking at houses— maybe tomorrow?"

"Sure." Tears welled as he left. Gabe had driven over to say good-night to his son. What a great guy. Gabe deserved to be a dad.

He deserved to be happy, to love and be loved. She couldn't stay, but while she was here she would help him however she could.

Chapter Six

"I'm sorry you're hurt, Eli." The hall clock had just chimed twelve noon the following day when Olivia finished pressing the adhesive strip to the child's arm. She winced in empathy at the ugly red scratches the length of his arm, but said only, "I'm sure it will heal quickly, honey."

"Thanks, Livvie." Gabe's son flung his arms around Olivia's neck and squeezed tightly, obviously needing comfort.

Maybe it was his use of her family's nickname, or perhaps it was the way Eli's hold tightened. Or maybe it was her own silly yearning to share a bond with this little boy. Whatever the reason, Olivia hugged him back despite her brain's protests. She was getting too emotionally involved, but she needed this contact as much as Eli did, needed it to soothe her aching heart. But what if—? She eased away from him.

"Don't climb on sharp rocks anymore, okay?" she advised, gulping down the rush of emotions his warm hug had caused.

"I won't." Eli's bottom lip trembled for a moment as

he studied the plaster bandage and the few angry red marks it didn't quite cover. Then he summoned a smile and, with shoulders back, pronounced, "I'm a big boy."

"You sure are, sweetheart." Concern for the children's safety made her ask, "Where were you playing, Eli?"

"There."

Olivia followed the direction of his pointing finger through the window. Every nerve went on high alert. There were no rocks over there, unless… She had to check this out.

"Show me exactly where." She followed Eli out of the office, her worry growing as they tromped through underbrush and straight to a pile of jagged rocks Jake had gathered from the property. "But there's a sign here, Eli. See." She pointed to each printed word, saying them distinctly. *"Keep out!"* She saw his blue eyes widen in surprise. "This little gate shouldn't be open. Did you do that?"

"Uh-huh." His head dropped to his chest.

"Why?" Olivia couldn't understand his disobedience.

"I needed a rock. Vic said we're gonna paint 'em after lunch." He frowned. "I gotta have a really nice rock. To give—someone."

A rock—the truth suddenly dawned. Sunday was Father's Day. Eli wanted to give his painted rock to Gabe. The significance of that action built a lump in her throat that she had to gulp down. Voice wobbling, she reached out and patted his shoulder.

"We'll find you a nice rock, Eli. But not in here." She firmly relatched the gate and double twisted the wire to make it very difficult to open. "When the sign says to stay out you must obey. The signs are to keep you safe."

"'Kay," he mumbled, eyes downcast. Something in his response bothered her.

"You did read the sign, didn't you?" she asked, but he darted away. She stood there, confused, studying the rock pile, trying to work it out.

"Something wrong?" Gabe's quiet question caught her attention. Olivia faced him.

"Do you think this sign is too small?" she asked, struggling to decipher a niggling warning that wouldn't be shaken.

"Hardly. You could read it from the kitchen window." When she didn't respond, Gabe set a hand on her shoulder, his voice concerned. "What is it, Olivia?"

"I'm not sure yet. I need to think about it some more." She forced a smile. "Ready to go house hunting?"

"Ready as I'll ever be." His tone made her do a double take.

"Are you getting cold feet?"

"No." His blue eyes held hers. "Just worried I'll miss some detail that's important to Eli."

"Then we'll take him—oh." Olivia stopped in her tracks. "He can't come with us today."

"Why not?" Gabe wore a confused frown.

"There's, um, an activity planned for this afternoon that he really wants to be part of." She shrugged. "It's not a problem. We'll scout out the houses and when you see a couple you think are suitable, we'll get his opinion. Not that I think he'll notice much except the windows. He's sure big on watching birds."

"Very big," Gabe chuckled. "When a bird arrives, he stops midsentence and stares. It's unnerving."

"Maybe we should find out what got him interested in them," she mused.

They walked to The Haven. Gabe said he'd have a word with his son while she got her purse. When Olivia returned, Gabe looked upset.

"What's wrong?" she asked. "Oh, you saw his scratches. Did you ask him about them?" When he shook his head, she explained what had happened.

"That's why you were asking about the sign." Gabe helped her into his truck, closed the door and walked to the driver's side. When the truck was rolling down the hill, he said, "Eli must have seen it. Why would he disobey?"

"We'll ask him later," Olivia temporized, not wanting to reveal the secret of Eli's Father's Day gift. "Now let's concentrate on finding your new home."

"I'm glad you're with me to help."

"Me, too." Olivia felt her stomach butterflies begin their dance at Gabe's grin.

This man was generous, kind, so loving to the son he'd only known for a few short weeks. Gabe was clearly a family man. It was such a shame he couldn't let go of the past and find love again. But no matter how much she wished it for him, Olivia simply couldn't envision exactly the right woman for Gabe.

Because you don't want to? Though she mentally scoffed at the thought, it persisted and wouldn't be silenced.

Delighted to see prospective customers, Harry St. Ames, the builder, took them on a tour of the yard where houses sat completed, waiting for families. Olivia tuned out the men's discussion about insulation and R-values of windows to scan the newest homes, comparing each to the vision in her head. The models that she'd shown Gabe online still seemed the best options, although she preferred one above the other. For now she'd keep that preference to herself.

"Roam around, look through each one," Harry invited. "Make sure you think about how you'll use your home."

They entered the first house. Olivia didn't care for the floor plan, but she followed Gabe without speaking, listening as he mulled over possibilities.

"I don't think this is it," he said after about five minutes. "What do you think of the one next door?"

"Let's look." She was determined not to reveal her partiality. Yet, as they studied the open plan, the large kitchen, the huge bank of windows off the living room and the sweet reading nook tucked into the corner, she couldn't help remarking, "Eli would love that spot. He loves it when someone reads to him."

"I noticed." Gabe mulled it over. "He doesn't seem interested in reading for himself, though. I remember when I was his age. I devoured books, even if I had to sound out every letter."

"Maybe when he has his own room, you can build a bookshelf and fill it with some of your favorite books," she suggested as they walked through the master suite.

"This is pretty nice," Gabe said with a grin. "Lots roomier than a bunkhouse."

They toured several other houses, however they kept returning for another look at the second one they'd viewed.

"I think this is it," the big cowboy said after they'd toured it again. "What do you think?"

"Let's walk through it one more time and see if we can find any faults," Olivia suggested, pleased that their tastes were so similar. "The kitchen seems perfect."

"Lots of room but still homey," he agreed. "Those windows will give a great view. I could stand at the island and look into the valley while I'm washing dishes."

"No dishwasher?" she teased. His droll look made Olivia chuckle. "The laundry room is handy. Which room will be Eli's?"

"He can choose, but I have a hunch he'll like this." Gabe walked into the blue bedroom. It featured a small turret-like jut out with a window seat beneath a huge window. "Plant a tree outside, set up a couple of bird feeders and it should have everything Eli asked for."

"Then I think this house is perfect for both of you," she murmured. "You can build a deck off the front from those French doors and enjoy your meals or a barbecue with friends."

"I never thought of entertaining." Gabe turned to stare at her. "But I could. Would you come if we invited you, Olivia?"

"Of course." The way he was watching her sent a tiny thrill up her spine, but it also triggered wariness. She didn't belong here, yet his words created an intimate picture that echoed a longing she'd kept suppressed inside since—no! Gabe was nothing like Martin. "You could watch a full moon and stars on a summer's night from the deck's vantage point."

"We could have fireworks in that valley on Canada Day. And I could put up a Christmas tree and decorations outside." Gabe's bemused tone made her smile.

"You can do whatever you want. It's your land and it will be your home."

"Home," he whispered. "It's been a long time since I had that." His eyes focused on her. "Thank you, Olivia."

He touched her cheek, the one with the scar, with his

fingertip, and for once she didn't flinch away. Couldn't. The intensity of his penetrating gaze held her in place.

"I don't think I'd have done this without you," Gabe said very softly. "I don't know how we'll ever repay you."

"Just be happy," she said around the lump in her throat. "Enjoy your home and Eli. That's payment enough." The quiet words slipped out. Her total focus was on Gabe, on how she'd only have to balance forward on her tiptoes to touch his cheek with her lips.

Been that route before, her brain warned. *Remember the pain.*

Only too well Olivia remembered gut-wrenching feelings of betrayal. But Gabe wasn't like that. Gabe had integrity and scruples. He wasn't trying to deceive her. She knew all about his world at the Double M, knew his friends, even his predilection for pie. He was everything she'd looked for in love and—

"Eve would hate this place."

That drew Olivia out of her daydream. Yes, she knew lots about Gabe, including his painful past. She especially knew how he was snagged in his anger toward his ex-wife. Everything in Gabe's world seemed tainted by angry memories of Eve.

Which was why Gabe wasn't interested in her as anything other than a friend.

That's what Olivia wanted, too.

Wasn't it?

Eve would hate this place.

As soon as the words left his lips, Gabe knew he shouldn't have said them and not only because the words cast a blemish on what had been a fun afternoon. Olivia's big smile had disappeared.

"Is that why you like it?" she asked.

"I really like the open layout and the way things seem to flow naturally. She liked—" He caught himself. "It doesn't matter."

"It really doesn't," Olivia agreed, her face somber.

"You want to say something." Because Gabe was learning to read her expressions he knew her next words wouldn't bode well for him. "Go ahead, Olivia."

"It's not my place," she began, but he shook his head.

"We're friends." He shrugged. "I know you're trying to help Eli and me. So be honest. Say it."

It took Olivia a few moments to summon her courage and speak.

"It's just—you keep bringing up Eve. Negatively," she added. Her soft gray gaze held his unrelentingly. "That can't be good for Eli. She was his mother after all."

"I don't speak about Eve at all around him," he objected defensively. Olivia cut him short.

"You do, Gabe. Not in words maybe, but in your manner. Whenever the subject comes up it's like an invisible cloak of fury falls on you." Her face seemed to soften as she stared at him. "I know it's painful for you, and I'm guessing that gets worse when you look at Eli and think about what you missed, what she took from you."

She saw a lot, this former foster girl. Maybe too much? Yet Gabe was determined to really hear what she was saying because this was about his son, the kid that he couldn't seem to relate to. And he wanted to—desperately.

"I'm not trying to negate your pain, but—" Olivia exhaled quickly as if for courage, then blurted, "I wonder if you're subconsciously holding Eve's misdeeds against Eli."

"That's not true!" Gabe stopped, reconsidered. Eli's words that first day replayed. *I prayed and prayed you would come.*

Why hadn't Eli said something to someone or run away?

Ridiculous! Where's an almost six-year-old kid whose mom is dying gonna go? To whom? That was why God made parents. All those years—why didn't you check on Eve? You should have made sure she was okay. It's your fault the kid had no place to go.

Gabe sagged. His fault? Could it be?

"I'm probably wrong," Olivia said somberly. "But your anger isn't helping ease the barrier between you and Eli."

"What do you suggest I do?" Gabe felt humbled and ashamed by her perception that he was the cause of the distance between himself and his son.

"Let's go get Eli, involve him in this." Olivia's silver eyes began to sparkle. "Somehow we've got to get that kid talking."

"First let me speak to Harry about buying this place. Then we'll go." Gabe wasn't going to dally over this decision any longer. That feeling of guilt and Olivia's insistence that they have their own house as soon as possible drove him. It made sense.

"Smart move." Her wide grin made Gabe even more certain of his decision.

When they returned to The Haven to pick up Eli, Victoria needed her sister's help. Rather than wait around until Olivia was free, Gabe thought of a plan. He whispered it to Eli and they left to put it into action, returning just before the supper hour.

"I wondered where you two had gone." Olivia ruffled Eli's overlong hair and smiled at Gabe. "Staying for dinner?"

"Uh, no." He didn't dare look at his son lest he blurt out their surprise. "We've had a look at the house. Now we're going out to the acreage to let Eli see how the house will fit there. Want to come?"

Olivia paused, glanced at the group of children filing into the house for supper and shrugged. "Sure."

Gabe caught himself grinning as he drove to what would soon become home. Eli, too, was smiling. For once they were going to surprise Olivia.

First the three of them walked the area. Gabe pointed out different aspects of the place to Eli, who seemed underwhelmed by the whole exercise.

"Is something wrong, son?" Gabe finally asked.

"There's no birdhouses." Eli's flat voice bothered Gabe.

"That's because we have to build them. But we won't put them up until they move in our house." Eli nodded as if he understood, but his gloomy look didn't dissipate.

New father or not, Gabe knew there was something else going on in that little head when the boy barely touched their surprise picnic for Olivia. Even she couldn't coax a smile from him. Her frown told Gabe she was as perplexed as he was by Eli's lack of response.

Gabe watched his son carefully while they ate their picnic. When he could stand the boy's silence no longer, he blurted, "What's wrong, Eli? Don't you want to live here? With me?" he added after a momentary hesitation. "You can tell me the truth."

Eli only stared down at his hands.

"You need to tell us what's bothering you, honey," Olivia encouraged. "If you don't tell us, we can't help."

After a tense pause that made Gabe clench his teeth, Eli spoke.

"How long will I live here?"

"How long?" Gabe figured he'd clearly overestimated his progress in figuring out this kid. "I don't know what you mean."

"This will be your home, Eli." Olivia's soft voice made Gabe think she was following a hunch. "It's going to be your home forever. Even when you grow up and someday move away, you'll always come back here because it's your home."

"I don't want to move away." Eli's ragged whisper tore at Gabe's heart. "I want to stay here and maybe—" He lifted his head and looked straight at his father. "Maybe I could learn how to work with horses, like you."

"Maybe you could," Gabe said around the lump lodged in his throat. "That would be a lot of fun."

"Yeah." Eli managed a smile and Gabe grinned right back. Progress at last.

But apparently Olivia wasn't satisfied. She touched Eli's arm.

"Tell me about your life with your mom, Eli," she said quietly.

The boy glanced at his dad half fearfully. A rush of shame filled Gabe. He'd put down Eve once too often for his son to be comfortable talking about her.

"We'd really like to hear," he said with a broad smile

of encouragement. "Where did you live? What did you do for fun? Did your mom have a job?" He kept his tone as neutral as possible.

"She had lots of jobs." Eli frowned. "It was nice when we had our own place. Sometimes we went to the park and I got to fly a kite." He smiled momentarily before it was gone. "Then we couldn't live there no more."

"Why was that?" Olivia voice was thoughtfully reassuring, the way a parent should be.

Gabe couldn't decide what she hoped to elicit from Eli, but he was content to listen and wait for answers. Maybe they'd help him understand his son better.

"When Mommy couldn't work we had to move out." A shudder rippled across his shoulders. "I din't like it then."

"Because your next home wasn't very nice?"

"We din't have no home," Eli said sadly, gazing into the distance.

"Oh. So where did you live?" Olivia glanced at Gabe, her gaze troubled. "With your aunt?"

"Not then. We stayed with some other people in funny kinda places. Sometimes we got to sleep outside. We had a big fire in a barrel when it was cold," he explained. His eyes lit up. "I liked that."

Gabe didn't. Was Eli saying they'd been homeless?

"A campfire *is* fun," Olivia agreed. "Could you cook hot dogs over that fire like we do at The Haven?"

"Mommy said no 'cause it smelled funny. Kinda like cars." He glanced at Gabe sideways, as if fearing his father would criticize his mother. "I had to stay with the loud lady sometimes 'cause Mommy was trying to get a job so we could find a place with real beds where it was warm and people didn't yell. But Mommy coughed too much."

"That must have been very hard, Eli. I'm sorry." Olivia hugged him close. "Were you hungry sometimes, too?"

"Uh-huh." He studied his shoes for a moment, then grinned at her. "But not when we went to the big church with the bells. We got to eat lots there. An' they had birds, lots and lotsa birds. A man in a funny dress showed me where the birds lived up in the bells. It was cool. I drawed a picture for Mommy, but Bobby teared it up." Again Eli glanced at Gabe fearfully.

"That's when you went to live with your aunt, right?" Olivia shook her head at Gabe when he would have interrupted. "Bobby and April are your cousins. Your aunt's children," she explained when Eli's face wrinkled in confusion. "I don't think they were very nice cousins, were they?"

Eli risked a quick look at Gabe before he shook his head.

"They were bad," he whispered. A tear fell from his downcast eyes. "But I din't tell."

"You can tell me," she murmured.

"Mommy had to go 'way 'cause she was sick. They said it was 'cause I was dumb, too dumb to help her. They said—" He sniffed and then a sob broke out. "They said I made her sick."

"But that's not right, Eli." An infuriated Gabe had to speak or blow up. "You didn't make your mom sick."

"I didn't?" Confusion filled Eli's little face. "But that's why Aunt Kathy said she had to lock me in the room an' I had to stay there all day 'lone. 'Cause I made Mommy sick."

"She was wrong, Eli. She lied." Gabe couldn't help it. He picked up his son and gathered him onto his lap. "I don't know why she lied, son. Sometimes people do that. But it was wrong, and it was not true. You are not dumb. And you didn't make your mother sick."

"How'd you know?" Eli's big eyes peered into his, waiting for an explanation.

"One time when we were married, your mom got sick. She had to go to the doctor because she was coughing so hard. The doctor told me your mommy had that cough for a long, long time, even when she was a little girl. He gave her special medicine that he said she'd have to take whenever she got the cough. You didn't make her sick, Eli."

"Oh."

Gabe couldn't tell whether it was relief or confusion flooding his son's face. All he knew was that he had to make this better, even though it meant praising Eve.

"You were a good boy and your mother loved you very much. It wasn't her fault that your cousins were mean. She wouldn't have left you there if she'd known about that."

Gabe suddenly recalled several disparaging comments his ex-wife had made about her sister and the treatment she'd received from Kathy when they were kids, before they'd both gone into foster care. Eve must have been desperate if she'd left Eli with Kathy. But why hadn't she come to him? If only— Anger made his jaw clench.

"Eli, when they made you stay in the room, did you miss school?"

Surprised, Gabe twisted to glance at Olivia. He'd never even thought of that. Eli slipped out of his grasp and moved about four feet away before he sank onto the ground, shoulders slumped in defeat.

"It's okay, son. It doesn't matter. We will—"

"Gabe?" Olivia's tone forced him to stop and look at her.

Those expressive eyes of her were trying to tell him something. But what?

"May I ask Eli a couple of questions?"

Hesitant, afraid he'd missed some key thing that he, the boy's father, should have noticed, Gabe nodded, and wondered, *What now?*

Fully aware of how important her next questions would be, Olivia sipped from her water bottle as she organized her thoughts. She had to ask, though she was almost certain she already knew the answers. The point was to get Eli's fears into the light where they could be dealt with.

"When you cut yourself today, could you read the sign that said to stay out?" she asked Eli after she'd shifted so she was seated cross-legged beside him.

"I know some of the letters," he mumbled, head hung low.

"But not how to make them words, right?"

He shook his head, obviously ashamed.

"Bobby and April said I'm stupid." A tear plopped onto his T-shirt. "I guess I am stupid 'cause I can't read words."

Olivia could feel Gabe's irritation building. She knew he wanted to gloss things over, make everything all right. What father wouldn't? But she knew that wouldn't help Eli.

"Am I stupid, Eli?"

"No." His eyes widened. "You're really smart, Liv. You do lots of things."

"Well, I can't read Spanish books, so that means I'm stupid, doesn't it?" She risked a glance at Gabe and saw his shoulders relax just a bit. "And I don't know how to make a spaceship or fly an airplane, so I guess I'm very stupid."

"No. You never learned that." He paused, staring at her as he absorbed it. "I never learned reading," he said slowly. "So, you mean—I'm not dumb?"

"Of course you're not!" He was so sweet. Olivia just wanted to embrace him and, like Gabe, make life perfect for this little boy. But she wouldn't be here long enough and besides, when she got involved with kids, bad things always happened.

"How're we gonna make me read, Liv?" Eli looked at her so trustingly. She couldn't disappoint him.

"We'll figure out something, don't worry. And don't be sad about it." She gave him her biggest smile and brushed his cheek with her knuckles. "April and Bobby should never have called you those names, but just because they did, it doesn't make them true. Okay?"

"Uh-huh." His big smile back in place, Eli jumped up and raced across the grass to inspect a robin's nest he'd spied earlier.

"Homeless. They were homeless, Olivia. Even then Eve didn't contact me." Lips pinched tight, his face taut with anger, Gabe glared at her. "I've never been without a place to live. Why didn't she call me?"

"She didn't know where you were? She didn't have money to find you? She was too proud?" Olivia shrugged. She had to make him understand. "It doesn't matter, Gabe."

"Doesn't matter?" He sounded outraged.

"No, it doesn't. There's nothing we can do to change the past, no way to find answers to your questions." She touched his arm, drawing his attention from Eli to her. "All we can do now is help your son. That means making sure he doesn't start school behind other kids his age."

"How do we do that? School will be out soon."

"He has to get to his grade level. I don't know how to do that, and I doubt you do, either. But I promise you this, Gabe. Getting that child ready for school is hugely important, if only so he won't feel he's what his cousins called him, what his aunt called him," she growled, a fierce protection rising inside. "Eli is not stupid."

"I thought the most important thing was getting us a home," he said, obviously confused.

"It is. But starting school at or above the other kids in his class will also help heal Eli's insecurities and help him settle into his new life."

"Olivia, I am deeply moved and very grateful for all your help with my son, but—" He frowned. "Neither of us know what or how to teach him."

"Correct. But I can find out who does." Her phone pinged. She checked her texts, then jumped to her feet. "It was a great picnic, but I have to leave. Now."

"What's wrong?" Gabe demanded, senses ramping to high alert. "Must be bad. Your face is pale and those tiny lines of strain around your eyes are back."

"Victoria fell while she was rock climbing. She's at the hospital. She has several broken bones, nothing life-threatening, but they'll put her out of action for a while." She stared at him. "The aunts need me to take over for her while she recovers."

"Okay." He waited. "Now tell me what's really bugging you?"

"I'm not sure I can do this, Gabe." She chewed her bottom lip, grateful she could talk this out with him before being inundated by her aunts. "But I can't say no, either. Summer is The Haven's busiest time. Disappointing all those kids who are planning to come?"

"You can do this, Olivia. You've already got the staff organized and scheduled. You've worked with Victoria, you know how things operate. And I'll do whatever I can." Gabe grinned at her. "I guess you won't be leaving here anytime soon."

"I—" She hadn't really considered what this would mean to her own plans.

"You'll be giving up your summer in Edmonton, but being at The Haven has lots of compensations." He grinned. "Including the kids you'll get to work with."

"Yeah." Olivia gulped. That was exactly what she was so worried about. She'd be the one in charge. What if she messed up and another child was hurt because of her?

When I am afraid I will trust in Thee.

I'm trusting You, God, she prayed silently as they drove back to The Haven.

At least Gabe would be around. The next few weeks would show if her judgment had improved, if the tall, lean cowboy really was a man you could count on if things got bad.

Don't let me mess up, she begged as worry filled her mind.

Chapter Seven

In Gabe's mind the July First Canada Day festivities at The Haven were a complete success.

Olivia seemed to have thought of everything and invited everyone in Chokecherry Hollow. The Haven was teeming. From sack races and fishing ponds to bouncy castles and a live theater presentation about the history of the Rockies, Olivia had planned something for every age.

For Gabe, however, the best thing was that he was part of it. Between watching and encouraging Eli's participation, Gabe judged several relay races, chose the winner for the bean bag toss and adjudicated the best-carved-watermelon contest. He didn't much care for helping with the face painting, but since there was a shortage of makeup artists available and an excess of children who wanted their faces decorated, and because he'd been promised a massive slice of lemon pie, he chipped in. Thankfully, the kids didn't care if his work was weird and lopsided.

Gabe loved being part of the celebrations instead of standing on the sidelines watching, as he had for so many years. Helping Olivia was an opportunity to pay back a little of what she'd done for him and Eli, so Gabe took the job seriously, ensuring she stopped for lunch, had coffee or a cool drink when she sagged, and insisting she take a few minutes to rest when possible.

Gabe also went to great pains to be ready to assist whenever he saw a tiny frown mar the smooth skin of her brow, whether that meant rescuing some weeping child or solving a new dilemma. By the end of the day he was weary but very pleased with his efforts and thrilled that Eli had enjoyed himself.

"You've outdone yourself today, Olivia," Gabe murmured as they sat together on a quilt hours later, watching the fireworks display. He glanced at his son sitting with Mikey. The two gaped at the colored flashes in the sky, oohing and aahing like everyone else. "Everybody enjoyed themselves, especially the kids."

"I hope so." She wrinkled her nose. "Thank you for saving my bacon with that bingo game. Don't ask me how I could have forgotten to get prizes," she muttered in disgust, cheeks pink. "My only excuse is that my phone went dead, again, which took out my schedule plan and I had to wing it."

"Which the aunts did very capably." Gabe chuckled, enjoying cool, competent Olivia's embarrassment. "The kids thought the ladies' prizes were fantastic."

"Except for Eli. I'm pretty sure he guessed I'd messed up after Aunt Tillie gave him her orange knitted hat." She winced. "At least he didn't tell everyone I forgot to charge my phone. I thought I'd done that last night, but—"

"Okay, your phone died. Cut yourself some slack, Liv. You did an awesome job taking over for Victoria. I doubt even she wouldn't have thought of throwing together that hike after you found out supper was going to be late."

Olivia shivered then so Gabe laid his jacket over her shoulders. True to form, this ultra organizer hadn't taken time to fetch a sweater for herself. She'd been too busy ensuring the kids were all warmly clothed and that her aunts were cozily ensconced in their lawn chairs with jackets and woolen blanket coverings to bother about herself. That was Olivia—selfless.

"That hike was not my smartest brain wave," she mumbled.

"What do you mean?" Gabe knew, but he sensed she needed to talk it out.

"That girl falling. That was my fault for letting her go along." She winced as the bang from a huge red fireball resounded through the valley. "Thank God you were there. I don't know what I'd have done otherwise."

"You would have picked her up, kissed her knee and carried on, of course. That's what you do, Olivia." He chuckled at her dour expression. "What?"

"I wouldn't have kissed her knee." She looked so sad he had to tease back her good humor.

"Because it was so dirty?" Olivia had a way of rolling her eyes that expressed her thoughts about his attempt at humor better than any words. Gabe tried another tack. "You'd have consoled her somehow if I hadn't been there."

She frowned. "I'm not very good at interacting with kids. I shouldn't—"

"Olivia, her falling was *not* your fault. She insisted on wearing those crazy boots despite your advice to wear sneakers. You kept checking that she'd suffered no ill effects and she, like all the others, had a great time dipping her toes in the stream." He chuckled, remembering the splashing. "On top of that, the hike helped them work up an appetite for Adele's delicious al fresco dinner. Couldn't ask for a better day."

"If it was, it was only because you and the aunties had my back. Thank you, Gabe." Her words sounded like a sigh as she leaned her head against his shoulder. "I couldn't have done this day without your help."

"That's not true," he insisted, liking the way her head fit against him. "Your middle names are *confidence* and *organization*. You're a natural at this job because you're a ways-and-means person. What you don't know you figure out."

"Ha! Look how I messed up with the kite races." She ducked her head so her reddened cheeks were hidden.

Gabe tried, but he couldn't suppress his laughter.

"It is *not* funny," she insisted, drawing away. "Someone could have been hurt."

"By a runaway kite?" He snickered at the disgusted look she tossed his way. "It's not as if you could have known the wind would kick up, Livvie. Nor is it feasible that one of those kids was light enough to be carried away by a gust of wind. Anyway, you soon got them interested in something else and it worked out."

"Yes," she murmured. "But next time it might—"

Gabe placed his fingertip against her lip and shook his head.

"'Sufficient unto the day is the evil thereof,'" he quoted as he slid his palm to cup her cheek. He winced when she immediately drew away, puzzled until he realized he was touching her scar. "Don't borrow trouble,

Olivia. Though if it does come, I still have every confidence in your ability to turn it into something good."

"Thank you." She tipped her head to study him in
the gloom. "You're a good friend, Gabe."

As they sat together watching the afterglow of the
fireworks die away, Gabe found himself disliking that
word. *Friend*. Somehow it didn't quite encapsulate
whatever this was that he and Olivia shared.

"Is that all there are?" Eli murmured after the last
boom. He yawned, then crawled into his father's lap.
Mikey was already asleep on their blanket.

"And now to bed," Olivia said as everyone around
them rose. "Is he asleep?"

"Pretty much." Gabe stood, hoisting his son into his
arms. "Feels like he's put on ten pounds. How much
watermelon did he eat?"

"Not enough. Adele says there are five of those monster things left over. We'll be eating it for days." Olivia
folded the quilt and slung it over her arm.

Ben had brought the aunties and Victoria to the site
in an ATV. Now, having retrieved Mikey, they were
loading everyone into the buggies for the return ride.
Gabe glanced at Olivia.

"Since they're full I guess we're walking back." He
didn't mind in the least that they'd have a few moments
together, on their own. Well, alone if you didn't count
Eli.

Gabe deliberately slowed his pace to allow people to
pass. With sunset falling soon after ten, parents were
anxious to tuck their children into bed. The counselors
from The Haven also shepherded their weary charges
toward their cabins. There would be no campfire to-

night. Everyone was worn-out. Except him. Oddly, Gabe felt completely alive.

"It was a perfect evening for fireworks." Olivia licked her fingertip and held it out with a grin. "Not even the tiniest breath of wind for the fireworks. Exactly what I prayed for after the kite fiasco."

"Proof that God answers even the smallest prayers." Gabe enjoyed the way moonbeams lit her expressive face.

"I like the way you include God in everything." Olivia's smile held a hint of wryness. "I try but often find myself fussing over things right after I've prayed about them."

"I'm no saint," Gabe protested, though he was flattered by her comment. "But his arrival," he said, glancing down at the boy sleeping in his arms, "has made me more aware of God's sovereignty."

Without a word spoken between them they entered The Haven, climbed the stairs and put Eli to bed. Gabe kept a close eye on Olivia as she tucked in the covers around his son, her hand lingering above his cheek before she quickly drew away. Something—longing?—washed across her face as she stepped back to give him room.

"Your turn," she whispered.

"Good night, son." Gabe brushed the flop of curls off Eli's forehead and pressed a kiss there, his heart full of love for this child, this blessing that had come from such a painful past. "Sleep tight." If only he'd been there from the beginning.

And the bitterness was back.

"Let's let him sleep." Olivia tugged on his arm, urging him from the room. She led the way downstairs and then outside to the patio, where solar lights beckoned them to enjoy the night's beauty a little longer. She sank into a chair and tucked her feet underneath her, her face troubled. "Just now, after you kissed Eli. You were thinking of her, weren't you? Of Eve?"

Gabe sat down across from her, uncertain of where this conversation was leading and uncomfortable with admitting the truth. "Yes."

"I could tell."

"How?" he asked, puzzled by her words.

"I don't know if I can describe it properly." Olivia shoved her hair behind her ear and leaned her head against the chair back to peer at the stars above.

Gabe doubted she realized her scar was clearly revealed in the moonlight.

"Try," he urged, liking that she felt comfortable enough to talk to him about it even though she knew he didn't. This must be important.

"It's not any one thing that gives you away, Gabe." She shrugged. "It's a combination of the way your face tightens, and you go kind of stiff for a moment, as if you're remembering she hurt you and are waiting for the next blow."

"That's a pretty apt description of how I feel," he admitted starkly. "How did you get to be so smart, Olivia?"

She chuckled as if he'd made a huge joke, but the laughter quickly died away as her face grew sad. "I know because that's how I feel sometimes," she confessed.

"When you get too close to kids," Gabe guessed, keeping his voice very quiet. "What happened, Olivia? Can you tell me what causes you to withdraw like that?"

Her internal fight was obvious.

But perhaps because she found her new job so stressful, perhaps because she was around children more than she had been, or perhaps because she was just plain tired of the past interfering with her present—whatever the reason, Olivia closed her eyes and began to speak.

"I was a foster kid for as long as I can remember."

Olivia blurted out the words, desperate to release the miasma of emotions whirling inside. She needed to talk to someone other than her foster sisters and her aunts. They were too close and might be hurt by what she so desperately needed to say.

Hurting those she loved was the last thing Olivia wanted. She knew Gabe would listen. His quiet "uh-huh" brimmed with understanding, proving she was right.

"All I know is that I was left as a newborn at the hospital in Edmonton with my name pinned to my blanket. I have no past, no history, no family. I have no memories and no records of who I belong to or where I come from. I just—" she shrugged "—am."

"But you've defined yourself since then, Olivia," he objected with a frown. "You've become a woman with a past, with history, with a family. You are loved. You belong at The Haven."

"I'm not decrying anything I've been given, Gabe," she assured him, striving to make him understand. "I'm just trying to explain how growing up was for me back then, how I always knew I never belonged anywhere or to anyone. That I always understood that wherever I was, it was only temporary. That it wasn't home."

"Until you came here." Gabe waited, frowning when she took a long time to answer.

"Yes." Olivia sighed. Maybe unloading on Gabe wasn't a good idea.

"I keep interrupting. Sorry. Please continue." Gabe's grin gave her the courage to push on.

"I was thinking. Maybe my lack of family history was the reason I always felt like an outsider, why I needed to belong," she murmured. "Without even realizing what I was doing, I began to define Olivia DeWitt by being ultra-responsible."

Gabe's empathetic nod helped her relax. His dark eyes revealed no condemnation. Just acceptance. Of course, that might change, but she had to take the risk. The feelings boiling inside demanded an outlet.

"In every foster home I looked for ways to make myself indispensable, to be someone they could count on in a pinch. So that they wouldn't want to let me leave," she added, aware that her tone had dropped.

"Understandable." Gabe grinned. "It also explains a lot about who you are now, Ms. Competence."

"Whatever. It didn't work, though, because I still got sent from one home to the next."

"Which meant you tried harder. You became increasingly responsible, maybe babysat even though you were too young?" He smiled at her blink of surprise. "Stands to reason and you are, above all things, a logical person, Olivia."

"I guess." She sighed, hating the next part. Though if he was to understand, it had to be said. "That's how I got in trouble."

Gabe arched one eyebrow in surprise, and suddenly she couldn't do it.

"This is silly. It's late. You have as hectic a schedule as I do." She jumped to her feet, forcing a yawn as if to prove her tiredness. "We should say good-night, Gabe. We can reminisce another time."

Only Olivia did *not* want to go back to that sad pathetic girl, to remember, to feel the guilt all over again.

"This is a perfectly good time. I don't have to be anywhere else." Gabe's steady voice told her she wouldn't get off so easily. "And I'm not in the least tired."

"You should be, after all the running around you did for me today. I do appreciate it, you know." She was surprised by the wry smile lifting his lips.

"Okay, you've thanked me profusely and used those good manners the aunts taught you. Now can you just say whatever it is?" he added in a soft murmur.

"I don't know," she admitted. "I'm—afraid."

"Of me?" he demanded, eyes wide with consternation.

"Not of you." Olivia wished she'd gone to bed and let sleep drown out the memories. "It's me. It's my past. It's—pretty bad," she warned.

"You were abused." The words sounded pulled from him. "Olivia—"

"No." She rushed to stop him. "That's not it. I almost wish it was."

"What? Why?" Poor Gabe looked so confused.

"If I'd been the one who'd been hurt, I could deal with that," she explained. "But to know that someone else was hurt because of me?" She shook her head. "That eats at me. You see, I'm the one who should have died."

Gabe stared at her. "I don't understand."

"How could you?" Olivia inhaled deeply, then sat

back down to quickly relay the details of her past, beginning with the fire when she was eight and then the drowning a year later. Accidents that had taken two of her young foster siblings.

She bared her soul, told him all the issues of blame and accusations that had followed, how the parents had hated her, because she'd lived and not their child. How after that she'd been shuffled from place to place, unwanted and in the way and growing increasingly bitter, acting out that bitterness until no one wanted her.

"I even beat up another girl once."

"You were an unhappy kid lashing out, Olivia," Gabe said softly.

"Yes. After those kids died—they sent me to therapy. I've been told many times by many people that those two deaths weren't my fault," she admitted. She lifted her head to study him. "It doesn't help. Psychologists, psychiatrists, counselors, ministers. They all say the same thing." Olivia made a face. "Forgive myself for not saving my foster siblings and get on with my life." She sniffed her disgust. "Trust me, I've tried."

"And?" Gabe frowned as he watched her face.

"I can't." She couldn't meet his gaze.

"Because?" As always, Gabe went straight to the point.

"Because I don't understand why I'm alive and they aren't. Because I can't figure out the reason they had to die and I didn't," she whispered brokenly. "They had family, people who loved them, needed them, wanted them. I didn't. I didn't matter to anybody. So why did God let me live? What's so special about me?"

"I finally get it. That's what drives your need to organize and find order. You're trying to make sense of your world." The understanding filling Gabe's voice made her study him. "You're trying to prove you deserve to be alive, Olivia."

"Am I?" She mulled it over. "Maybe. I am trying to be the very best I can be."

"Because?" He was pushing her to look deeper.

"It's stupid, but if I'm good enough—" Olivia hesitated, his gaze holding hers "—maybe then I won't be responsible for another child being hurt?"

"That's why you avoid kids, to protect them." Could he see into her heart? "And that's getting harder to do because you've taken on Victoria's job and responsibility for kids scares you. It's like being thrust into your childhood again." His dark eyes glowed. "Am I right?"

"I've always tried to do my best, Gabe." She reconsidered her life in Ottawa. "I volunteered where I could. I tried to make my life meaningful…" She let the sentence trail away, hating the pathetic sound of desperation in her words.

"All of that is great, Olivia." Gabe crouched in front of her. His hands closed over hers, warm and comforting. "But you're putting too much pressure on yourself. You can't keep living your life avoiding contact with kids without it adversely affecting you. And what you're saying now proves that is already happening. You're constantly checking yourself lest you get too close."

"Avoiding them is the only way I know to protect them from me. What else am I supposed to do?" Tears rolled down her face. "Tell me, Gabe, and I'll do it."

"You can't *do* anything to fix the past, Livvie—" He stopped and shook his head. "You have to let it go."

"How?" she demanded, angry that he made it sound so easy.

"By accepting that the deaths of those two kids so long ago were not your fault." His unflinching gaze held hers. "There's a verse I really like from Psalms 56. 'What time I am afraid, I will trust in Thee.'"

"I've tried that," she muttered. "Repeating biblical verses doesn't help me."

"Of course not." He chuckled at her glare. "Because repeating them doesn't reach the heart of the issue. You have to *believe* the words you're repeating." He reached up to brush a wisp of hair from her eyes. "Sweet Olivia, you're trying to take responsibility for something that's not in your power."

"Huh?" She struggled to concentrate on what he was saying, too aware of his warm fingers and how much she liked his touch against her skin.

"Those children living or dying—whether *you* lived or died—that was not your decision, Liv." Gabe's gentle voice soothed as much as the brush of his fingertips. "Trusting God means believing He knew what was happening, He was there, and *He* decided when those children died. It was never up to you. You mattered to somebody. You mattered to God and He wanted you to live. It was His choice."

"But maybe if I'd—" The big strong cowboy's gentle fingertips smoothed across her lips to stop the words.

"Uh-uh. You don't get to second-guess God's choices," he said in the most tender voice she'd ever heard. "God never put young Olivia in charge back then. He knew you wouldn't save those two kids. He didn't expect you to. He doesn't expect that now, either."

Olivia remained still a long time, long after he drew his hand from her lips.

"Then what does He expect?" she asked miserably.

Chapter Eight

Olivia's words fell like raindrops, almost silent in the hushed evening. But in them, muted though it was, Gabe heard her unspoken desperation to be free of the long-time load of guilt she'd been carrying. He sent a silent prayer heavenward for the right words to offer this precious woman.

"I think He expects you to trust that He had and still has it all under control, to rest assured that He has a plan, even though it's one you may never understand." Gabe felt as if he was treading on shaky ground. He was no Bible scholar, no expert on the thoughts of God. But helping Olivia understand that she couldn't keep blaming herself for the heartbreak of her past was like a physical need inside him. This beautiful woman's sadness reached in and gripped his heart so strongly it scared him.

"Continue, Gabe. Please?" Her trusting silver-gray eyes gazed into his and he knew he had to keep going.

"Either you believe God is in control of everything, or He's not in control at all. There's no halfway with trust." He had to get this right, had to help her understand. "Either you believe God does what is best for us or…"

Gabe deliberately let it hang, praying that she'd finally absolve herself of the blame. But Olivia wasn't there yet.

"It sounds too easy to just blame it on God's will," she murmured.

"Not blame. Trust." Gabe's emotions were running wild. He couldn't stay so close to her, but he couldn't walk away, either. He'd sort out these crazy reactions later; now he needed some space between them. He rose. "The past, as painful as it was, happened. You can't change it. But you can change your future."

"How?" she demanded with a glare.

Typical of this organized woman. She needed a plan, an organized, detailed strategy. But most of the time life didn't have one.

"Trust," he said gently, watching as the words penetrated. "Stop being afraid."

She was silent for a long time. Gabe glanced at his watch. It was after one in the morning and he had a full riding day tomorrow. He should get home. And yet he was loath to leave and end these special heart-sharing moments with Olivia.

He was about to say good-night when she spoke.

"Is trust how you recovered from your divorce, Gabe?"

There was no malice in Olivia's question, but in his head her words condemned his self-righteous advice, because even after all these years he still could not get past Eve's perfidy. Though she was no longer alive, his anger at her would not abate. It was a familiar ache. Too familiar. Why couldn't he forget her?

Gabe did not want bitter thoughts of Eve to taint this special new relationship with Olivia, so he brushed it off with a glib response.

"I'm still working on the trust part. Maybe I always will be." He cleared his throat. "I need to get home and you need your rest. Good night, Olivia." He turned to walk away, but suddenly Olivia was there beside him, touching his arm.

"I didn't mean to hurt you, Gabe," she said, her voice gentle. "I'm so sorry if I did. You've been a great friend to me. Thank you." She wrapped her arms around his waist and hugged him with a fierceness that surprised him.

And yet it felt right. It felt as if Olivia *belonged* in his arms. Without a second thought, Gabe embraced her, holding her close in the intimacy of the evening's darkness.

"I know you're trying to help me and I appreciate it," Olivia whispered into his shirtfront. "But I don't think I'm going to be able to trust God very easily."

"We all work at it," Gabe murmured into her hair, noting the fresh citrus scent of it even after a hot day spent racing around The Haven. "But the kids that come here need you, Olivia. They need your leadership, your perspective, but most of all, your love. You've been where they are. You can empathize with their struggles as no one else can. Maybe that's why God brought you home to The Haven."

"Just temporarily." She burrowed closer.

Somewhere in the hills surrounding them a coyote howled. The trees rustled with a light breeze that rifled through her hair, tossing those strands against his cheek. Gabe lifted one hand to smooth the silky threads, filled with awe at the wonder of God's creation, and of this special woman who thought he was some sort of hero.

As if.

"Maybe you don't know your family history, Olivia, but you know God." Gabe rested his chin against her hair. "You've known Him for a long time, haven't you?"

"I thought I did, but—God doesn't change, so I guess you're basically saying that now it's time to put my faith where my mouth is." She drew away, sobering. "It's time for me to walk the faith I talk. I agree with you. It's way past time."

Gabe's arms felt empty now that she'd stepped back. Odd how absolutely *right* that embrace had felt when he'd sworn he'd never let a woman get close again.

He so did not want to think about Eve now. Yet he'd chastised Olivia for her lack of trust. Was it the same for him? Did he doubt God's ability to heal his heart? Was he clinging to the anger because he was afraid God would let him get hurt again?

What about Eli? This was no time to be thinking about romance. Not when Gabe still hadn't figured out fatherhood.

"Gabe? What are you thinking?" Olivia watched him with those all-encompassing eyes that took in far more than anyone realized.

"That tomorrow's going to be here before we know it," he growled. "And that you don't need any beauty sleep, but I do."

True to form, Olivia tilted back on her heels to study him. "I think you're very handsome."

"Sure." He brushed the words aside like a joke.

"I mean it. You're a very good-looking man, Gabe. But what I like best is that there's more to you than simple good looks. You have a quality, an inner integrity, that drives most everything in your life. You're utterly honest and that's refreshing. Lots of men aren't who you think they are."

Meaning the guy she'd fallen for, the one who already had a family? Comparing him to that creep did not sit well with Gabe.

"Don't crown me yet. The reason I don't tell lies is because you always get caught." He shrugged, brushed her nose with his lips, then stepped back. "It's late. I have to go. See you tomorrow."

"Good night, Gabe. And thank you again."

He nodded. He didn't want Olivia's thanks.

What did he want?

Gabe walked to his truck, climbed inside and drove away, knowing she stood there watching until he disappeared from her sight.

I don't tell lies, he'd claimed.

Yeah, right, cowboy. You're telling the biggest lie of all and it's to yourself. If you told the truth, you'd have to admit that hanging on to your anger at Eve allows you to forget that not everything about your marriage was awful, and that some of the awful part was your fault. You didn't love your wife enough and that's why she left.

Uncomfortable with that, Gabe tried to put the past out of his head by mentally forming a list of all the things he needed to do before the house was moved at the end of the week. It didn't work.

In the wee hours of dawn, he was still wrestling with the bitterness that wouldn't go away.

"C'mon, Livvie. I got my stuff. We gotta go see my house moving." Raggedy suitcase bumping against his skinny legs, Eli tugged at her arm, urging her toward the car.

"It won't be there yet, Eli. Houses get moved slowly." She smiled at the excitement blooming in his face. So like Gabe. One fingertip touched her cheek, remembering how he'd held her. *Stop it!* "Do you like going to Miss Erma's now?"

"Yeah. At first I didn't want to go when you tol' me 'bout her. But she's nice an' she has lotsa games," the boy said. He threw in his suitcase, then buckled himself into the back seat. "I really like games."

"I do believe you've told me that once or twice," Olivia teased as she checked the belt, then fastened her own. "Which game do you like best?"

"The cookie game." Eli giggled when she rolled her eyes.

"Figures. My sister says you're like the cookie monster in her kitchen." Judging by the chocolate smear on Eli's shirt, Olivia figured she'd probably hear it again.

Olivia had discovered Ms. Erma Nettleworth's private tutoring class thanks to the aunties. Though neither Tillie nor Margaret had said so, Olivia was almost certain the two ladies had been instrumental in helping retired teacher Erma start her remedial summer learning program. Newly widowed, Erma was struggling to pay down the mortgage on the lovely cottage she and her late husband had built for their retirement. Her program was fast gaining notoriety for her unique and extremely effective methods of helping kids succeed scholastically, and Eli loved it.

Thrilled that Gabe's son would start school well-grounded in the basics and that she'd been able to talk Erma into taking one more student under her already bustling wing with the simple exchange of a week at The Haven for her grandson, Olivia reveled in a rush of joy. Finally, after all Gabe had done for her, she'd been able to do something to help ease his burdens. Now if she could only find a way to erase the tight lines around his mouth whenever he mentioned Eli's mother.

Half-listening to Eli outline how Miss Erma's cookie game worked, Olivia drove to Gabe's acreage while hoping she'd covered all eventualities that could occur at The Haven in her absence. The staff were rock-solid, and her earlier insistence that they be able to take over different facets of the ministry when Victoria couldn't be there was beginning to pay off, as was her hard-fought scheduling plan. Olivia was mostly happy with that part of her job.

She wasn't as satisfied with her own efforts at running her aunts' program. That kid, Skylar—she'd let him go on the ride today even though she'd known in her heart of hearts that he was lying about his previous riding experience. She'd purposely questioned him several times and watched him carefully on the ride yesterday, expecting trouble. Since he'd done all right, she couldn't very well hold him back from going with his group this afternoon, but—

"Liv?"

"Yes, sweetie?" She glanced in the mirror at the young boy who'd wormed his way into her heart despite her resistance to getting too involved with him.

"D'you think I'll like it in my new house with… Gabe?" That slight hesitation was painful to hear after all this time, but it also told her Eli had been thinking about this for a while.

"Don't you?" she asked.

"I dunno. It's kinda funny." He kicked his sneakers up and down for a minute while he thought about it. "I never had a whole house of my own before."

"Funny good?" she asked.

"I guess." He didn't sound convinced. It would be up to Gabe to prove it to him.

"I'm sure you and your dad will have a great time in your new house."

"Yeah." Eli's bottom lip trembled. He dashed a hand across his eyes, then turned his head to stare out the window. "My mom won't be there," he whispered.

"No, she won't." Uh-oh. Olivia pulled into the yard site and parked well beyond the area needed to manipulate Gabe and Eli's new home into place. "But she'd want you to be happy with your dad. She'd want you to enjoy your new house and all the birds that will come."

Eli looked at her as if he thought she was making it up. "How do you know?" he asked when she got out and began undoing his seat belt.

"Because she told your aunt that you were to come here and live with your dad. She wanted you to be happy, so she made sure your dad would look after you." Olivia stopped herself from hugging him though her heart yearned to ease his sadness. "You told me about all the things your mom did. I think she always did her best for you, didn't she?" She waited until he'd nodded his head. "Oh, sweetheart. I wish she could be here to see you now, to watch you riding a pony and learning to read and flying that kite. She'd be so glad to see you being happy."

"But if she was here—that wouldn't be good." Eli stopped, a catch in his voice. "My dad hates her."

"Oh, no, Eli. Gabe doesn't hate your mommy." Olivia paused. She had to get this right.

"Well, he gets a mad face when I talk about her. An' when I tol' him the funny story about how one time our popcorn got burnt on the fire, his hands went like this." He formed his little hands into fists.

"Sweetheart, I'm going to tell you something. You'll have to be a little bit grown-up to understand, but you're so smart, I think you can do that." Olivia exhaled, hoping she was doing the right thing. *Help me*, she prayed silently.

"Well? Tell me, Liv." Eli's scared voice emerged in a whisper.

"I will, but I was thinking that first we should get out our blanket and sit on the grass. We can watch while we talk." When they were seated on the hillside with the house-moving panorama spread out before them, she tried to explain. "Your mom and dad got married when they weren't very old. They didn't know lots of things about being married so I think they made lots of mistakes. Those mistakes hurt your dad. Sometimes people can't forget getting hurt by somebody they love."

"Huh?" Eli's confusion had her sifting through her brain for a better explanation.

"It's like with you and Mikey," she said, wondering how she'd gotten into this. Involvement so wasn't her thing. And yet… Trust God, Gabe had said. "You two are good friends, right?"

"Uh-huh. 'Cept when he tells me I gotta do sumthin'. I don't like that."

"I understand." She smiled. "I think it was kind of like that with your mom and dad. He loved living on his ranch because he really likes horses. But maybe your mom never lived on a ranch before. Maybe she was used to living in town and she didn't like having so much change. Some people don't."

"Oh." Eli's tanned forehead furrowed as he considered that.

"Maybe your mom and dad couldn't agree about lots of things. That would make it hard to live together. Maybe they argued. Lots of people do and that makes being together even harder, like when you and Mikey argue and then you don't want to play with him for a little while."

"The man in my class at church said you're not 'sposed to argue," Eli muttered, peeking at her as if he wasn't sure he should mention that. "God doesn't like it."

"God doesn't like arguing," Olivia agreed. "But sometimes people get angry and they do argue. Sometimes they stay angry." She could almost feel herself drowning here and all because she'd taken on the responsibility of this child. *Not your business*, her brain reminded. But she'd started. She had to finish it.

"You mean my mommy and him din't want to fight so they din't live together no more?" Eli slowly put the pieces together.

"You'd have to talk to your dad to know for sure, but I think maybe that's what happened," she said, wincing at her oversimplification. "But people change. Just because your mom didn't like to live on a ranch back then doesn't mean she wouldn't like it that you're here now, Eli."

"Really?" Hope made his eyes glow.

Keep going, something inside Olivia encouraged. *Make staying here with Gabe in this house okay for him.*

"I'm pretty sure that if your mommy could see you

and your dad living in this new house and enjoying it, she'd be very happy."

"How'd you know, Livvie?" he asked, big eyes searching hers for assurance.

"Because moms always want the very best for their kids, and this place, with all its trees and birds, plus a snug house that will keep you warm in the winter— I think this is the kind of place that would make your mom smile." She waited, breath suspended.

"She liked trees an' grass." He sniffed, then nodded. "An' she liked to be warm. She *was* scared of horses, but maybe she'd get used to them, like me," he said hopefully.

"I think so." Olivia loved that Eve had showered her love on this little boy. Poor kid. How awful to be left totally alone with his horrid cousins after knowing his mother's wonderful love. "It might take some time to get used to things with your dad, but I think you're going to like it here, too, Eli. Let's ask God to help you."

She quietly prayed a blessing on Eli and his dad.

That done, they shared a smile as they sat together, surveying the area below them. The burnt-out shell of the old house had been completely removed since Olivia had been here last, and a new cement pad poured. Assorted mechanical pipes and outlets awaited hookup. Her gaze automatically searched for and found Gabe. He spent ages speaking with someone, but then he waved and jogged up the hill to talk to them.

"Very smart to park over here, Olivia," he said after ruffling Eli's hair. "It's well out of the way." He crouched down and explained to Eli what was about to happen. Then he produced a small camera, a sketchbook and some pencils. "I thought you might like to make some memories of today."

"Thank you." Eli listened to his explanation about the camera, took two practice shots and then assembled his pencils in perfect order. After a second look at the site, he began to draw.

"That's a great idea, Gabe." Olivia admired his tall lean figure in the bright sun. This cowboy always looked ready to handle anything which was just one of many things she admired about him.

"He's always reciting memories about Eve. I want to have a record of our memories together, too," Gabe murmured, his gaze meeting and holding Olivia's. "Thank you for bringing him. I know you have a lot on your plate, but I appreciate you taking the time to be here with him."

"Well, of course I want to see your home moved in." Why did it feel as if his blue eyes saw past her bland comments to the nervous quiver in her stomach? "It's a big day for you both."

"It is." His gaze shifted to Eli, who was busily re-creating the gorgeous summer afternoon with swift, sure pencil strokes. "The first of many. I hope."

"Hmm. Who was it lecturing me about faith—was it only last week?" she asked, miming an innocent blink.

"Guilty." Gabe shrugged. "I'm trying to do better, but I'm a work in progress."

"Me, too." She shared a smile with him before someone called and he strode away as the first truck bearing a wide-load sign rounded the bend. "Here it comes, Eli."

They sat entranced as the white house rolled into view. After much discussion, various movements backing up and going forward, the house was finally ready to be moved onto its footings.

"It's perfect," Olivia mused to herself as it slowly, gently moved over the ground. She felt an undue delight in how the house didn't take away from the stunning landscape around it but made the entire setting more beautiful.

"It belongs here, right, Livvie?" Eli said softly.

"It belongs, and so do you," she said with a gentle smile. "You and your dad."

Eli tipped his head back and stared at her without saying a word. But Olivia was getting better at translating the expressions fluttering through the dark eyes so like Gabe's. She saw hope and longing in those dark eyes. Then Eli focused on the movers.

"What's that big hook for? An' why do they have ropes? An' what does that yellow machine do?" His questions came at a rapid pace as he snapped pictures, but Eli quickly grew disgruntled with her lack of illuminating answers. Eventually, he stopped asking.

"Don't you have any more questions?" Olivia studied the little boy who was always curious.

"I'll ask my dad." He offered her a glance brimming with pity. "You know lotsa stuff, Livvie, but I don't guess you know much about moving houses."

"I guess I don't," she admitted, and tucked her smile behind her hand.

It seemed to take forever before the house was finally settled in place and being expertly fastened down. Olivia had brought along two bottles of juice, an apple and a granola bar, which she and Eli shared as the afternoon grew warmer. Gabe, she noticed, never seemed to pause in his inspection of the house, constantly checking that everything was done correctly.

The afternoon grew late. Olivia knew it was time for her to get back to The Haven and her job, but she couldn't just leave Eli. A quick check via her cell phone ensured no one had left a message about any major issues. Maybe she could stay a little while longer.

To pass the time, Olivia made up a game where she quizzed Eli on the letters he'd learned, made up words with them, then watched him painstakingly print them on the tablet Gabe had given him. Finally, the movers seemed to be finished. They left just as a huge truck drove in.

"What in the world—?"

"It's our stuff." Eli jumped to his feet in his excitement. "We got lotsa things. I even got a bed with drawers underneath it. Can we go watch them put it in my room?"

"*Your* room, huh?" Delighted that he'd laid claim to his new home, Olivia thought about it for only a moment. If they needed her at The Haven, they'd call. "We'll ask your dad."

Worried he might rush into the chaos of vehicles, Olivia took his hand and they walked toward Gabe. Well, she walked. Eli almost danced. It was the most excited she'd ever seen him.

Inside Olivia was dancing, too, because finally Gabe would be home with his son.

By the time Eli went to school she'd be leaving. The thought sobered Olivia like a douse of cold water.

But she didn't want to stay.

Did she?

Chapter Nine

Gabe divided his time between watching the men load in furniture and housewares and watching Olivia and Eli. But mostly he watched Olivia. He wanted—no, needed to see her approval for his choices, though he wasn't exactly sure why.

"My son's bedroom first," he directed the movers. "Then he can be in there while we fill the rest of the house."

As promised, the men assembled the captain's bed and put it in place. A chest of drawers, a small desk and a chair followed.

"Gabe, you had them build in a window seat for Eli!" Olivia's gray eyes shone like polished silver as her fingers brushed his arm, though he knew she wasn't aware she'd done it. "It's perfect."

"There should be a cushion—ah. There it is." He took the long, tailored rectangle and, enlisting Eli's help, set it in place. "Try it out, son," he encouraged, loving the sound of that word "son."

Eli carefully took off his sneakers, then climbed onto the seat and peered out the window.

"It's good," he said. "But there's no tree."

"Not yet. You and I will plant one this weekend," Gabe promised.

"An' then the birds will come." Eli stared at him so trustingly. Gabe vowed then and there that he'd never do anything to betray that trust. "An' birdhouses?"

"Soon as we build them." He ruffled Eli's already messy hair before asking, "Eli, can you do your drawing in here while the movers bring in the rest of the furniture? I don't want you to get hurt by something."

"I'll draw stuff," the boy said proudly. "Then we can hang it on the wall."

"Good idea. Call out if you need anything." Gabe doubted that would happen soon since Eli seemed enraptured by his new surroundings. He sprawled across the bed, tried out the desk, raced to the window seat and then started all over again.

Gabe surreptitiously beckoned to Olivia to follow him.

"What can I help with?" she asked as they stood behind the kitchen island watching the movers carry in furniture.

"How about if you tell me if you think things need to be moved around?" he suggested. "That chair, for instance. I'm not sure—"

"It's a bedtime story chair," she told him without batting an eyelash. "It should be by the fireplace. No, that table can't be in front of the windows. It blocks the view."

Gabe smiled to himself. Olivia had told him she'd help find the house but that she would not get involved in decorating it, and yet here she was, directing the movers to rearrange his purchases in a much better configuration than he'd come up with. Exactly what he'd wanted.

She caught him smiling and blushed.

"I'm so sorry, Gabe. I didn't mean to take over. Wait," she called to the moving men, but Gabe shook his head. "It's perfect as it is," he told them.

Wrought iron stools fit perfectly at the kitchen island, and even better, they were heavy enough that Eli could climb onto them without fear of tipping. Appliances, bedroom furniture, a table and chairs, two loungers for the patio—all were set in place and, where needed, connected.

"The water should be hooked up by now," he told Olivia. "But it will take a bit for the hot water tank to reach capacity, so I'll have to wash our new bedding later." He grinned when she pointed to a box that sat in a corner. "That's Eli's, but he's not getting it. Not yet." He stopped her from calling out to Eli with a hand on her arm. "They have to put up the blinds. Then he can open it."

Gabe almost laughed out loud at the curiosity filling Olivia's expressive face. He wondered when the last time was that this ultra-organized woman had been kept in suspense. Following on the heels of that thought was a decision to arrange a surprise for her before she left.

"Everyone moves so fast." She watched as the blind hangers finished in the living room and kitchen and moved on to the rest of the rooms. "You can hardly tell anything's there," she marveled, trying to peer behind. "How do they work?"

"Remote control." Gabe loved seeing her astonished face when he pressed a button and the shades on the massive living room windows lowered. "I can even program them to close when I'm not here. And I had a skylight installed in my bathroom that will close at the first sign of rain."

"Wow. You're a surprising man, Gabe Webber." She looked suitably impressed.

"Because I bought a house with some toys?" He made a face. "Well past time, don't you think?"

Just then Amy Andrews, the daughter of local hardware store owners, pushed her way inside, lugging two gigantic boxes.

"Let me help," Gabe insisted, and lifted them from her arms. "More?"

"In the truck," she said with a grateful smile.

"You start unpacking. I'll bring them in." He glanced at Olivia. "You could help Amy, if you want."

"Sure." She opened one box. "What have we here?"

"Kitchenware." Amy grinned. "Gabe wanted his home functional from day one."

Satisfied that he'd surprised Olivia, Gabe began carrying in Amy's boxes. When he returned with the final box, Olivia had found his dishes.

"These are my favorite pattern," she told him, fingering the pale gray-on-white check. "They fit in perfectly with the decor."

"He said they reminded him of you." Amy chuckled as Olivia's brows rose. "I understand what he means now. It's like you said, Gabe, dainty but sturdy." She continued working, apparently unaware of Olivia's red face. Soon the island was laden with what she'd assured him were necessary kitchen essentials. "How do you want these things organized?"

Gabe blinked. Though he hadn't a clue, he knew who would.

"Ask Olivia," he suggested. "She's the most organized person I know."

"But it's your house, your kitchen," Olivia protested.

"And I'm asking for your help. I'm going to check on Eli." Gabe knew that if he left, she'd take over, so he stayed away a good half hour, grateful for the precious moments of sharing time with his son. They discussed all the things they would do together in the future.

Then they went outside together to watch as the last details on the house were completed. Finally the seller, Harry, handed over the keys.

"Welcome home, Gabe. You too, Eli," he said with a grin for the little boy. "I hope you enjoy your new home."

"Thanks a lot. We appreciate everything." Gabe shook his hand firmly. "Buying from you was so easy. You made the sale a pleasure."

"A lot of that was due to Olivia, you know. She's the most detailed person I know. Even gave me a checklist." Harry chuckled. "It was a good one, too."

Gabe was surprised by the information, but then he realized that's what she did. She'd been part of this from the beginning. Of course, she'd want to ensure the move went smoothly. For Eli's sake.

Gabe and Eli sat on the patio and chatted about birds and bugs and bedtime. Then he remembered Eli's box.

"Let's go inside." His heart racing with anticipation, Gabe glanced around.

The kitchen was now completely organized. Everything seemed to have a place, and the whole effect was bright, cheery and efficient. Though his appliances, large and small, were all in a stainless finish, there were bright splashes of orange here and there. Amy had asked his preference for accessories and he'd blurted orange because it made him think of Olivia. She always wore an orange scarf, an orange hair clip or some other item in that shade.

Gabe saw a bright orange pitcher and matching glassware behind the glass-doored cabinets. He didn't remember buying that.

"Amy says those are a thank-you gift from her parents," Olivia explained. She looked perfectly at home seated at his kitchen island, laying out bright orange woven place mats on the white stone counter.

"To say thank you for your business," Amy explained with a wide grin.

"Thank *you*. Both of you. What you've done looks amazing," he complimented, overwhelmed by his magazine-worthy kitchen.

"It's mostly Olivia's doing. I just put things where she said. Now I must go. Thanks, Gabe." After a wave at Eli, Amy gathered up her three bags of packing refuse and left.

"Hey, Eli. What's up?" When Eli shrugged Olivia glanced at Gabe.

"It's time for Eli's box." Smothering his excitement, Gabe picked up the box and carried it to a spot on the hardwood floor not covered by the new area rug. "This is for you, Eli."

"It's not my birthday yet," his son protested.

"It's for all your birthdays when I wasn't there. And Christmases, and Easters." Gabe stopped because the same old surge of anger at Eve blocked him from speaking. Enough! He was not going to allow it to ruin this moment. He cleared his throat. "It's from me to you."

"Th-thank you." But Eli just stood there, staring at the box.

Gabe hadn't anticipated his uncertainty, wasn't exactly sure about the proper way to handle it. He shuffled awkwardly until—

"Don't you want to see what it is?" Olivia walked to a corner of the rug near the box and sank onto it. "I do. Come on, Eli. Open it."

"Okay." Still Eli hesitated. Then he moved next to Gabe and slid his hand into his father's. "You help," he said quietly.

"We'll do it together." His heart so full it felt like he'd explode, Gabe sank down beside Eli and removed the first piece of tape, then let him do the next.

"It's a—a train?" Eli lifted his head to stare at Gabe. "It's old."

"Just like me," Gabe told him with a grin. "It was my grandfather's and then my dad's. They both passed it on to their sons and now I'm passing it on to my son. You."

"Oh. Thank you." Eli carefully lifted out one piece after another, examining each thoroughly before moving on.

"What a great idea, Gabe," Olivia whispered. Gabe saw tears in her eyes. "A welcome-home gift from father to son."

"How does this train work?" Eli asked, both hands full of train tracks.

"Let me show you." Gabe lay on his stomach and demonstrated how to put together the antique train that he'd once loved so much. He got it running and then Eli took over, laughing out loud every time the engine whistled and the caboose rattled around the track. Gabe moved to sit beside Olivia, content to soak in the sight and sound of Eli enjoying something without reservation. A muted noise made him glance at Olivia. He quickly did a double take.

What was the woman bawling about?

"What did I do wrong?" he demanded with a frown.

"Nothing. You did everything perfectly." She leaned over and kissed his cheek. "You've done a wonderful, wonderful thing here, Gabe. The house, Eli's room, the window seat. That's amazing. Passing on a bit of his history to give him a sense of connectedness, to make him feel he belongs—it's the perfect end to a wonderful day."

With Olivia's head resting on his shoulder and his son giggling nearby, Gabe thought so, too.

Nearly perfect.

Only—what was he going to do when Olivia left for her new job and he was all alone?

Olivia cradled her cup of mint tea against her cheek and sighed. Mid-July. She loved this time of year.

She also loved that The Haven's latest youth group was gathered in the meadow below them, joyfully belting out songs as they roasted marshmallows over the campfire. Seated beside her on the patio, Gabe stretched out his long legs.

If only…

"Why the frown?" he asked.

"I thought it would get easier," she admitted softly, hesitant to tell him that.

"Hasn't it?" He studied her. "You looked very competent and in command today when you were organizing the kids into search teams for that girl who wandered off."

"I wasn't competent. I was a nervous wreck. It didn't help that my stupid phone died again."

"The new battery didn't help?"

"Maybe I didn't let it charge long enough," she admitted sheepishly. "I do know that I've never in my life prayed so hard as I did today. The relief of finding Sara lying in that field of wild clover, studying cloud shapes…" Olivia rolled her eyes, fairly certain her heart rate would never be normal again. "I had to give her a lecture about wandering off. This place is fenced, but that doesn't mean wild animals don't occasionally get through. What she did was foolhardy. And against our rules."

"Agreed." He arched one eyebrow. "But you straightened that out, didn't you?"

"As best I could, though I'm not sure I got through. Her reason for needing space didn't make sense to me. As usual. I just don't 'get' kids sometimes." Olivia tried to stifle her feelings of inadequacy.

"But it wasn't just Sara, was it?" Gabe asked.

"No. Skylar acted up again. He got into a fight with Jeffry, who is the sweetest kid." Olivia pursed her lips. "This is Skylar's third visit here, and I honestly don't know why that center in Edmonton keeps asking if he can return when we have to keep reporting his misbehavior. I don't think he's learning anything from being at The Haven."

"He's probably learned way more than you realize. They all have. You *are* making a difference here, Olivia. Even if you can't see it right now." Even in the gloomy twilight, Gabe's smile blazed white. "God's using you. All you have to do is trust."

"Now where have I heard that before?" she muttered,

then slumped, ashamed as silence stretched between them. Gabe was always so encouraging. It wasn't fair to unload on him just because things hadn't gone according to her plan. "Sorry."

"Hey, I can take it. But I hate to see you so down. And grumpy," he added with a cheeky grin.

"Lately I'm always grumpy," she admitted.

"No, you're not. What's changed?"

"Nothing." *Everything.*

He just kept staring at her, waiting. Olivia sighed. It was useless to prevaricate. Gabe could see right through her.

"Today Victoria told me she needs additional physiotherapy, in Edmonton. That means I'm going to be running this gig for at least another month."

The thought of overseeing so many children for even one more day set her teeth on edge. She'd accepted that she would have to stay at The Haven until her sister was able to return to work. She'd tried hard to trust God knew what He was doing sending the toughest kids here. But she'd never imagined she would be in charge for so long. That she hadn't yet goofed and ruined some kid's summer seemed like it was only a matter of time.

Besides that, Olivia still didn't have a place to live in the city, nor had she done any background work to prepare for her new job. She was worn-out, unsettled and totally out of her groove. And she didn't like those feelings. They reminded her too much of her past.

"You know you'll miss The Haven and the kids when you leave, Liv. But it's not really about this job, is it?" Gabe's blue eyes held hers, waiting.

"Not totally." She checked over one shoulder to be certain there was no one to overhear. Then she admitted in a quieter voice, "Managing the office is fun. I feel competent, like I can do it with one hand tied. But problems with the kids—that drains me. I'm totally, utterly ill-equipped to handle all the issues that keep cropping up."

"Discipline, you mean?"

"Not just that. Some of these kids are very troubled. They need someone to talk to, someone to advise them." She chewed her bottom lip. "How can I be sure I'm not making things worse for them?"

"The fact that you're even asking yourself that question is a great sign." Gabe shrugged. "You're smart and resourceful, and I doubt you have to worry. But you do have trained counselors you can call on if you need to. You're not alone in this." His mouth quirked into a smile. "You know what I'm going to tell you."

"Trust God." She let her breath out in a whoosh. "Easy for you to say, buddy. You're getting a handle on your world. You're all moved into your gorgeous new house and you told me you now have full legal custody of Eli. By the way, where is he tonight?"

"Home. I put him to bed before I came over. Amy's child sitting. I've been told she's very trustworthy." Gabe frowned. "But don't think everything's right in my world just because I'm in a new house, Olivia." His lips tipped down. "I have my own battles to fight, one of them being Eli's continued silences, even when I offered to get him a pony. The kid just won't confide in me the way he does with you."

"Maybe he's still scared of horses," she offered.

"Doubtful, given his over-the-top response to riding the miniatures at the Double M last weekend. It's something else." His jaw clenched. "I think it's tied up with Eve."

"Eli mentioned her the day you moved in." Olivia relayed the conversation as best she could remember. "It seemed to me he was feeling guilty because she isn't here and doesn't get to enjoy his new home."

Given Gabe's glowering expression, it probably wasn't the right thing to say, but she was tired of skirting around this issue.

"Look. If you want Eli to open up to you, you've got to encourage him to talk, no matter what the subject. And you have to listen."

"I already do that," he shot back sharply.

"Really? Well, if you get all tense and angry like you are now, it's no wonder the kid clams up. I'm no child expert, but even I can see that." She wanted so desperately to help this sweet, kind cowboy, but there was only so much she could do if he wouldn't break free of his cycle of bitterness. "Sooner or later you *are* going to have to forgive her, Gabe."

"I've tried, but—I don't think I can." The whisper-soft confession was punctuated by his bowed shoulders that expressed his defeat. "Believe me, I'd love to be free of the memories of what she did, to stop thinking about how much time I've lost with him, to stop mourning all the things we never got to do together. But I can't. What am I supposed to do?"

"I don't have the answer." Olivia's heart ached for his obvious pain. "I guess we have to keep praying for God to intervene, to work it out in your heart. Otherwise—" She was not going to finish that.

Gabe did.

"Otherwise I'll never get to be the father I want to be,

to have the relationship I want to have with my child," he finished. "I know Eli's probably the only kid I'll ever have, and everything's so messed up with him." Gabe now looked angrier than before.

"You know that's not what God wants. Trust that He has something better planned for both of you. But you have to do your part, too, Gabe." She leaned forward, earnestly desiring to help him.

"What's that?" He glared at her.

"Stop dwelling on it. Every time a negative thought comes, confess it and give it to Him. Don't cling to it and rehash it over and over. It's done." She knew her situation wasn't the same, but she was desperate to help this man she liked. "I was talking to the aunts this morning about how inadequate I feel to deal with these kids, how much I want to escape when they come to me with their issues. The aunts gave me a verse. Maybe it will help you, too."

"I'll accept all help." Gabe shuffled his feet on the patio, obviously restless.

"It's from James, first chapter, verse five. 'If any of you lack wisdom, let him ask of God, that giveth to all men liberally, and upbraideth not; and it shall be given him.'"

He mulled it over while Olivia studied him, loving the way he was so determined to be the father Eli needed.

"You don't know how to rid yourself of the bitterness, Gabe, but God does. Ask Him to show you."

"I'll try," he said, but there was an edge to his voice that told her he didn't think it would be that easy.

The group in the meadow was climbing up the hill toward them now, heading for their cabins and some rest. Olivia wanted that, too. She'd been woken before four this morning to drive a sick child to the hospital and the lack of sleep was catching up.

"You're yawning," Gabe said, a smile in his voice. "I should go. Amy's curfew is soon."

"Okay." She rose and found she was very close to him. "Try not to worry too much," she consoled quietly. "I doubt God would have brought Eli here if He didn't mean for the two of you to be happy together. Hang on to that."

"I guess." He stood blocking her way, thoughtfully studying her face. "Ever wonder why He brought you here, Olivia?"

"To step in for Victoria," she said more airily than she felt. There was something about being so close to Gabe that was unsettling, though why that should puzzled her. He was the best friend she'd ever had.

"A stand-in? You think that's all God intended?" His tone amused, Gabe fiddled with his black Stetson. "In working on the trust factor, one thing I've noticed is that God often has something else going on. We think it's about one thing, but it often turns out to be a much wider scope that we thought."

Olivia couldn't smother another yawn. She blinked in surprise when Gabe bent and brushed his lips against her scarred cheek.

"Good night, Olivia. See you at church tomorrow."

"Good night," she finally managed to whisper, but Gabe was long gone. And so was her tiredness.

She went inside to retrieve Aunt Tillie's bilious purple afghan, wrapped herself in it and curled into the big wrought iron chair on the deck to think about what Gabe had said.

She *was* only staying at The Haven to fill in. She certainly didn't belong here. She wasn't sure she belonged in Edmonton, either, but that's where her new job would take her.

"I don't know about the future," she murmured long after the kids had retired and only the night sounds of the woods echoed around her. "But now that I'm here, I want to do what I can to leave a mark on these kids' lives. Please show me how to do that."

Gabe's handsome face, hurt and angry, swam into her mind.

"And please help Gabe. Show him a way to forgive Eve so he can concentrate on his future with Eli. Use me to help them if You want."

Olivia wasn't exactly certain why she felt compelled to ensure the father and son's reunion. She only knew she wanted the very best for them.

"Help us both to trust You, Father."

When Olivia finally climbed the stairs, she felt a new courage infusing her. There would be more tests to come, but with Gabe's, the aunts' and her sisters' help, by trusting God to guide her, surely she wouldn't mess up any of the troubled kids who came to The Haven.

"On my own I probably would fail, maybe even endanger some kids," she whispered. "I'm scared stiff I'll do that anyway. But You must have me here for a reason. Can You give me some clue to what that is, please?"

Olivia's sleep that night was fitful. She fell into a dream where Gabe and Eli were playing a game outside their new home. Somehow it was a sad dream.

Because she wasn't there.

Chapter Ten

"Today we're going to see the school you'll attend when summer's over." Gabe studied his son's bent head, bothered that Eli barely looked at him. "Aren't you excited?"

A shrug.

"Well, I am. I believe you're going to enjoy meeting all the kids and teachers and learning new things." He paused, waiting for some reaction.

Eli lifted his head to study his father. For Gabe, it was like looking in a twenty-five-year-old mirror. Strange how much Eli looked like him, and yet, had he ever been so...closed up? He had to get Eli talking.

"Did your mom ever talk to you about going to school?" Eli's nod made Gabe purse his lips. Would this child ever speak normally, blurt out things like other kids did? Why was it always such an effort to get any information about the past? "What did she tell you?"

Eli took his time answering. "To not be scared," he finally murmured.

"Why would she think you'd be scared of school?"

And why did a comment from Eli about Eve get Gabe so bent out of shape?

Eli stared at him for a minute, then returned to eating his cereal. "I dunno," he whispered, tucking his chin into his neck.

From Eli's reaction, Gabe immediately guessed that he'd said something wrong. Or done something wrong. But what? *Oh, Lord, I just don't get this kid.*

In his brain he carried on a conversation with Olivia.

You have this tone when you speak about Eve, Gabe. Her brows would be drawn together as she studied him with that penetrating silver gaze.

What tone? Did he have to be so sarcastic?

That tone you just used with Eli. Olivia would glare at him. *Eve's gone, Gabe. She can never be part of Eli's life again.*

Thank you. I had realized that, he'd shoot back, irritated by her criticism.

Then why are you so afraid, cowboy?

The question ended his pretend discussion. He wasn't afraid.

Was he?

"Is Livvie comin' to my school with us t'day?"

The question drew Gabe out of his contemplation and annoyed him.

"Olivia's working at The Haven today, like she always does."

"Oh." Eli's shoulders sagged until he was almost hunched over, like a fearful little ball.

Feeling like a bully, Gabe was ashamed.

"She couldn't come to our supper last night, either," Eli murmured. "I wish she coulda."

"I'm sure she wishes she could have, too. But she

had an emergency, remember?" He remembered how excited Eli had been to serve the meal they'd prepared, recalled, too, how utterly devastated Eli had been when Olivia phoned to say she had to return a homesick child to Edmonton. So now Gabe repeated the paltry words of comfort he'd offered last night. "Olivia can't help it if she has to cancel her plans. Sometimes some of the kids she works with need her."

"I need her, too." At least that's what Gabe thought Eli mumbled.

"Won't I do?" he asked, gutted when Eli shook his head in a firm no. "Is it private?" He hated that Eli would keep something private from him.

"Kind of. Sometimes I tell Livvie 'bout stuff." Eli peeked at him, as if worried his father would object to that.

"I'm glad you can talk to her, son." Gabe couldn't discourage Eli from speaking to the one person he trusted, but he felt compelled to warn him. "Olivia's helped us both an awful lot because she's our friend. But the thing is, she's very busy. We don't want to take up too much of her time."

"Isn't Miss Victoria's leg never gonna get better?" Eli asked, his frustration evident.

"It will. But it takes time. So Olivia has to do all the things Victoria would do. Because we are Olivia's friends, we don't want to make even more work for her. Right?"

"I guess." Eli blinked, but Gabe figured he'd understood most of it.

"That's why I don't want to ask her to come on our tour of the school today," he explained. *Also because I'll be better able to focus on what your teacher's say-*

ing if Olivia isn't there to distract me. "Maybe we'll have time to stop at The Haven. Then you can tell her about it before you go to Ms. Nettleworth's place this afternoon. Okay?"

"Okay." Eli's eyes blazed. He straightened up, finished his cereal and tucked the bowl into the dishwasher as Gabe had shown him. "Should I go brush my teeth?"

At Gabe's nod, Eli dashed away to complete the task. Gabe squeezed his eyes closed.

Eli's not the only one who wants to see Olivia. So do I. But every time I'm around her I get all these feelings and it reminds me of the past. I don't want that to happen again.

Please, God, help me understand how to deal with this churn of emotions inside.

I can't love Olivia!

And yet he did. The knowledge had been lurking in the corners of Gabe's brain for a while now, waiting for him to stop lying to himself. He was in love with the lovely organizer. But he didn't want to be, didn't want his heart vulnerable, and he sure didn't want to ever feel that gut-wrenching sense of betrayal again. Bottom line, Gabe did *not* want to reexperience the weakness that love brought. The cost of being vulnerable was too high.

But what he wanted didn't seem to matter. He still loved Olivia. He tried to push it away.

Okay, so he was supposed to forgive Eve. He'd talked to the aunties by phone yesterday, told them the whole ugly story. The aunties had texted later offering their sympathy but insisting that God expected Gabe to forgive Eve. They said only forgiveness would get rid of this iron lump of anger festering in his gut. But how exactly was he supposed to do that when even her name made him uptight, never mind thoughts of her betrayal with Eli?

Olivia would tell him to suck it up. No-nonsense Olivia. Even thinking about her made him smile. She'd become such an integral part of his world. Of Eli's, too. In fact, she was the one who made Gabe's world with Eli work. She was the buffer between them. The odd day when he didn't see her seemed gray and lackluster. Olivia made life worth living.

He loved her.

Stunned by the absolute rightness of that thought, Gabe swallowed the rest of his coffee. But the dark bitter brew couldn't erase the truth that rang through his brain. He loved her, but he would never act on it.

And yet—life without Olivia? He couldn't wrap his brain around that without his stomach sinking to his feet.

Unsettled by his inner conflict, Gabe drove Eli to the school. The tour explained who his teacher would be and which rooms Eli would be in, however, none of it dislodged his thoughts from Olivia.

Sweet Olivia, who feared getting too involved with any of The Haven's youth lest she hurt them. Olivia, who went out of her way to keep from hurting everyone. Olivia, who put her heart and soul into whatever she did.

Gabe drove Eli to The Haven with his jaw clenched, feeling caught between a rock and a very hard place. Yes, he loved her. Seeing her was like having the sun slide out from behind a cloud.

But love was a vulnerability he couldn't afford. The cost was too steep.

"So how did school go?" Olivia smiled at him, then hunkered down to Eli's eye level.

"Okay." Eli eyed the picnic table loaded with food and drink, then surveyed the kids lounging around enjoying their lunch. "Can I have some of that?"

"Of course. Help yourself." She waited till he hurried away. Then she scowled at Gabe. "What happened?"

"Nothing. We went to the school, Eli met his teachers, saw where he'd be sitting, and we left." Gabe itched to follow his son and sample some of those golden chicken drumsticks before they disappeared, not because he was hungry but because that would put some distance between him and Olivia. Maybe then he could convince his brain that he couldn't care for her. "It's all good."

"No, it isn't." She glared at him. "Eli's not talking, not even to Mikey, and Eli always talks to Mikey. What happened?"

"Nothing." Gabe edged toward the table. "Can I beg some lunch, too? Once I drop Eli at Ms. Nettleworth's I'm going to have to work double time to catch up on my chores if I am to take that group of yours on a ride."

She stared at him. Gabe could feel her gaze probing his soul.

"Chicken," she accused darkly, glaring at him.

"Olivia—"

"Forget it. I don't want to hear your denials again. Go eat." She waved a hand. "I can talk to Eli later. On second thought, maybe I'll get something, too. I missed breakfast."

Once again the familiar concern for her he so often felt flared inside him.

"You can't afford to do that, Olivia," Gabe chided. "You've got to keep your energy up."

"What energy?" she muttered, rolling her shoulders as if to ease tension. "I think I'm too old for this."

"Eat. You'll feel better." The mundane subject allowed him to breathe. When Olivia put so little on her plate, Gabe piled up a second one to temp her. He followed her to an empty table away from the mayhem and watched her sink onto the bench.

"What I really want is this tea. I'm so thirsty." She sipped the icy beverage, ignoring her plate, and closed her eyes. "Perfect."

That's when Gabe noticed the two dots of color on her cheeks.

"Are you feeling all right, Olivia?" he asked.

"No. I think I'm getting a cold. A summer cold. The worst." She wrinkled her nose in disgust before taking a tiny bite of carrots. "Also, I messed up again. One of the counselors believes I erred by not hugging Skylar after our latest discussion, the one where he agreed, again, to follow our rules."

"What difference would you hugging him make?" The remark irritated Gabe. Olivia didn't mess up. She was meticulous about her work and he hated that someone dared criticize her and made her doubt herself. "You were trying to make Skylar realize that he and everyone else have to obey the rules. That doesn't require hugging."

"She suggested hugging him might get through to him better than lecturing him." She gave him a dour glance, silver-gray eyes narrowed when he snorted in disgust. "She's a counselor, Gabe. She's had lots of training. I'm sure she knows more about kids than I do."

"Maybe," he allowed. "But not about running The Haven. You're taking care of every aspect that has to do with these kids because that's your job. Hers is to work directly with the kids." He noticed that she kept glancing around, scanning the children. Something else was going on. "You're worried. About anything specific?"

"No." But he knew she was because her gaze rested a long time on the boy named Skylar.

"Stop worrying." Gabe held out his extra plate. "Eat."

"Yes, sir." She made a face, but when he continued to hold out the plate, she finally took half a sandwich and a slice of watermelon. After sampling each she grinned. "Thanks. Guess I was hungrier than I thought. What's your afternoon look like?"

"Same old." Gabe shrugged, not wanting to tell her of his phone call to the aunties. Then he'd have to tell her that this morning's conversation with Eli had shown him he was a fool if he kept believing everything was going to work out. Gabe prided himself on not being a fool.

Clearly the past was coming between him and Eli, and even though Gabe wasn't convinced it was possible to forgive Eve, he was beginning to accept that he had to try.

"I'd better get Eli to Ms. Nettleworth's," he said after checking his watch. "Thanks for lunch."

"No problem. See you later?" When Olivia smiled at him like that, brushed his arm with her fingertips as if she really did want to see him later, Gabe felt strong, important, confident—all the things a man aspired to be, if only because he wanted to be worthy of a wonderful woman like her. All the things Gabe wasn't because he couldn't get past his past.

"Yeah." He savored one last look at her lovely face, then went to find Eli. And maybe later, when he returned, he'd have another chat with Tillie and Margaret. There had to be a way to forgive Eve, even if he didn't want to.

Olivia watched Gabe leave. She wanted to call him back but then decided she had nothing to substantiate her concerns about Skylar. Gabe was an expert with horses. He would handle whatever the boy threw at him.

Thrusting aside the worry that had clung all morning, she returned her dishes to the kitchen, checked with Adele about the trail ride dinner planned for tonight, then took attendance of each child climbing onto the bus that would drive them to the Double M ranch to attend Gabe's riding group this afternoon.

Skylar smiled as he passed her. If there was acrimony on his part, it didn't show. Olivia silenced her concern as she watched the bus leave. There was a lot to do today. She didn't have time to waste on what-if.

She spent the next two hours teaching a class on hand-building pottery. What a pleasure to instruct the three girls who seemed to have no ulterior motives.

"You've done a great job," she congratulated, admiring their displayed items. "Now you need to smooth off the edges more because when these dry, they'll be very difficult to work on."

"How fast will it dry?" Sari, a bright-eyed girl who'd blossomed into a chatterbox after the first two silent days, asked.

"Typically, we'd cover it tightly and then smooth it off in several stages as it slowly dries. But with this heat and all the wind we've been having, I'd suggest double covers. Tomorrow it should be dry enough to skim off a first layer. If you leave it too thick it will probably crack."

Olivia loved teaching pottery. She'd offered this hand-building class because she'd noticed that as The Haven's ministry grew, some youth didn't wish to pursue riding. Some needed more personal attention or were unable physically, and some were eager to learn hobbies that they could hopefully pursue at school later.

That's why she'd persuaded Aunt Tillie to teach a knitting class and, after much coaxing, gotten Adele's agreement to give simple cooking lessons. Olivia strove to find each child's niche in hopes they'd eventually open their hearts and share their struggles.

Olivia was becoming more comfortable in this area as she realized The Haven's ministry wasn't about her fears, but about the troubled kids who came here, about reaching them however she could. Now she was learning to pray for guidance, shove back her hesitation and grasp whatever opportunity she found while God worked things out. Slowly she began to enjoy the challenges, though each day was still a test. But thanks to her fosters aunts' support, she was learning how to be used.

The pottery girls' giggles filled the air. Fresh scents of mountain wildflowers and Adele's delicious baking tickled Olivia's nose. The murmur of her aunties' voices as they shared tea on the patio—all these things made Olivia aware of how bleak and barren her former life had been. Avoiding kids, pouring her energy into organizing to forget her past and the guilt that still lurked in the nether regions of her mind—those past actions had never tested or fulfilled her like this work.

In her new job there would be no concerns about

whether a child needed someone to listen, whether she'd failed a needy child, caused a problem or endangered some poor kid. Maybe she wouldn't have to trust God as much, either.

Silly little daydreams about staying at The Haven had filled her head lately. Not just because then she'd see Gabe constantly, or for the blessing of having her family's fellowship every day, or for the delight of watching Eli grow, but for reasons that encompassed everything about this place. She loved it here.

She couldn't stay, she knew that. Victoria was in charge. There wasn't enough work for them both and, anyway, Olivia didn't belong here. She wanted to belong with Gabe but that, too, was a pipe dream. But couldn't she at least stay long enough to see just one of her labors succeed? To see one child completely change for the better?

When she was gone, would the dreams stop? Olivia wondered. Dreams of Gabe and his life with Eli in their snug new home, sharing all their father-and-son firsts— first day of school, first Thanksgiving together, first Christmas. Sadness engulfed her knowing Eli would forget her as he built his place in the world, a world she wouldn't be part of. And Gabe—did he ever wish she'd stay, be part of his world permanently? Of course that was silly. Gabe was still stuck in the past.

The girls laughed and worked together on their clay, leaving Olivia with her thoughts.

Would Gabe miss her? When the stars came out and he needed a second opinion, would he find someone else to bounce ideas off of? Would he care if he never saw her again? Would he keep praying for her after she left? Would the bond they'd built hold up when she came back for Christmas, Easter, the aunts' birthdays? Probably not.

But Olivia knew now that wherever she went, part of her heart would remain here with Gabe. The realization that she was falling in love with him had dawned slowly over the past few weeks. Now it was rooted deep inside. Gabe was the man she loved, the real love of her life. She desperately wanted him to love her back.

Olivia knew Gabe cared for her. But each time she thought he'd finally declare his love, his bitterness against Eve came between them. She knew his long-held bitterness wouldn't let him trust her, not as a man should trust the woman he loves. The way she yearned to be loved.

I guess I need to learn to trust You with Gabe, too. She smiled sadly. Everywhere she turned the lesson was trust.

"Olivia? I think something's wrong." Sari's troubled voice drew her from her thoughts.

Jake, The Haven's hired man, raced toward their pottery shed. Olivia hurried to meet him.

"What's wrong?" she demanded.

"Don't have all the details," he huffed, trying to catch his breath. "Gabe phoned, said a kid, Emmet, fell off his horse and hit his head. Gabe's at the hospital. It had something to do with that kid, Skylar."

"I knew he was up to something." Olivia glanced at the girls. "Can you girls clean up? Jake will help you store your pieces and take you back to the main buildings."

"We know what to do in an emergency because you made us practice." Sari grinned cheekily. "Go. And send Skylar home." She was one of the kids Skylar had publicly mortified.

"Jake?" Olivia glanced at the hired man.

"Go," he ordered.

Olivia hurried to her car, praying as she went.

Please take care of Emmet. I'm trusting You, she repeated over and over, but every time she said *I'm trusting You*, her heart sank a little further.

I should have stopped Skylar.

Chapter Eleven

Where was Olivia?

Gabe paced the hospital corridor, thankful his boss, Mac McDowell, had insisted that copies of permission slips for every rider from The Haven be kept on file at the ranch. Being able to bring it along meant there had been no delay in treatment of this kid.

"Gabe?" Olivia raced toward him, hair flying back, her scar puckered and reddened against the whiteness of her face. "What happened?"

"That kid, Skylar, loosened the cinch on Emmet's saddle. They'd just begun to canter when someone yelled and next thing I knew Emmet was lying on the ground. He hit his head on a fence rail and cut his hand." He grabbed her shoulders and hung on, hoping to soothe the terror he saw written on her face. "Emmet's fine, Liv. The doctors are with him. I only brought him here as a precaution. I called but your phone is off," he added, knowing he sounded testy.

"No, it isn't—" She dragged her phone from her pocket and stared at it. "It's dead again."

"You need a new one." *Nothing like stating the obvious, cowboy.*

"This is the second new battery I've put in it. I'll order a new one tomorrow." She shoved it back in her pocket. "Skylar again. I thought that kid was up to something."

"Wish I'd—" Gabe cut himself off when the doctor appeared.

"Emmet's fine. He'll have a bump on his noggin, though. I want him to rest for another fifteen minutes before he leaves. The nurse will give you a list of things to watch for. Nothing serious, just precautionary."

Gabe listened as Olivia extensively questioned the medical professional, like an overprotective mother. He finally intervened so the doctor could answer a page.

"Emmet's fine." He blinked in surprise when strong, capable Olivia's face crumpled. She threw herself into his arms and started crying. "Hey. It's okay," he murmured, smoothing a hand down her shiny hair. "It's all good."

"It's not good at all," she sobbed against his chest. "I knew Skylar was up to something."

"You couldn't know that, Olivia," he protested, loving the way she fit in his arms. Where she belonged.

"I knew. He has this way of looking at you," she asserted, lifting her head to frown at him. "When Skylar's smile doesn't reach his eyes, trouble always follows. I've seen it before and I should have warned you."

"Olivia." She moved as if to pull away, but Gabe held her arms.

"Yes?" She looked at him in puzzlement.

"How could you have warned me?" He had to reassure her that no one could have foreseen the boy's actions. "What would you have said? Be careful. Watch out?"

"Maybe." Frustration chewed at the edges of her response.

"But we were already doing that. Every time we allow someone to sit on our horses we do that. We check and double-check. We always watch as closely as we can," he insisted.

"I know. But—"

"No." Gabe shook his head. "You can't be their babysitter, and neither can we, Liv. They have to follow the rules. Unfortunately, they suffer the consequences if they don't."

"But that's just it. It's not Skylar suffering," she shot back with a glare.

"Isn't he?" Gabe raised his eyebrows. "Isn't that why he keeps acting out? Because somewhere inside him something hurts, and he can't make it better? Because he needs you and The Haven to help him figure it out?"

"I'm not good at figuring out kids or trying to be a parent." Tears streaked her lovely face as she gazed at him. Her voice dropped to almost a whisper. "I want to be. I wish so desperately that I could be like their mother and protect them. But I'm not. I'll never be a mother."

That threw Gabe off balance. He'd never suspected to hear such a depth of longing in Olivia's voice, never suspected that she yearned to be a mom.

"Why not?" he demanded. "You're great with Eli. You're great with the kids at The Haven. Just because you had a tough childhood doesn't mean you wouldn't make a great mother, Olivia."

"Two kids died, Gabe."

"Stop," he snapped, hating to see her suffer. "Both were accidents. Let go of the past." The funny little smile tilting up the corners of her mouth surprised him. "What's funny?"

"This advice of yours." She shook her head, eyes crinkling at the corners. "Earlier today I was thinking the same thing about you."

"Huh?" Olivia thought about him?

"Do you remember when Eli started to tell you about his mom and you cut him off? Your anger at Eve always gets in the way between you and him," Olivia said in a very quiet tone. "I'm wondering why you don't let the past go, just as you've told me to do."

"It's not the same."

"Isn't it?" Her honest stare made him flinch. "Things happen to all of us. But I'm learning the past is past. You and I can't change it. If you want a future with Eli, you have to let the past go." Her smile darted back to her lips. "I do, too."

He loved that about Olivia, her chipper, take-it-on-the-shoulder-and-come-back-fighting air that squared her posture and lifted her determined chin. But it was her silver-gray eyes that wouldn't let him off the hook.

"I can't. It keeps coming back," he muttered.

"Because you let it." She eased away from him, tossed her head and blew her nose. "I've been doing the same thing with my fears. But I'm not doing it anymore. Life's too short to be constantly living in the past."

"Meaning?" He didn't think he liked where this was going.

"I have a job to do for as long as I'm here. Then I'll move on. I believe that's God's plan for me and until He shows me differently, I'm committed to obeying Him. The aunties texted me a verse this morning. 'For I know the thoughts that I think toward you, saith the Lord, thoughts of peace, and not of evil, to give you an unexpected end.'" She tugged her shirt and straightened her shoulders. "I've got to believe God will keep His word. So no more weeping, no more whining over the past for me. It's time, past time, for me to trust God completely."

"That's what I love about you, Olivia." The words tumbled out of Gabe before he could stop them. Stunned and a little embarrassed by them, he hurried on. "You never run away from challenges. You keep pushing forward. You're an admirable woman."

He stared at her, mesmerized by her quiet beauty. Then, without conscious thought and following an overwhelming impulse, Gabe leaned forward and kissed her the way his heart had been demanding for weeks now. Olivia startled, then eagerly responded. Gabe eased his arm around her waist and drew her closer, deepening the kiss as he tried to show her how much she meant to him, completely forgetting his vow not to love.

When Olivia's arms twined around his neck. Gabe thought he'd never been happier, until someone cleared their throat.

"Sorry." The amused nurse couldn't conceal the glimmer in her eyes. She winked at the boy standing beside her. "Emmet has been discharged. You may take him home."

"Thank you." Olivia slipped away from Gabe and knelt beside the little boy. "I'm so sorry this happened, Emmet."

"It was Skylar's fault," the boy insisted quietly.

Gabe frowned. Emmet didn't sound angry or upset with Skylar. He wondered why. Apparently, Olivia did, too.

"What do you think I should do about that?" she asked.

Emmet took his time considering while the nurse ushered them out of the hospital. He walked between Gabe and Olivia across the parking lot, his dark eyes narrowed.

"You gotta talk to him and find out what's making him so mad," Emmet finally suggested. "'Cause that's why he does stuff."

"You are a very smart boy, Emmet." Olivia brushed her hand over his bristly hair. She smiled at Gabe, then her eyes widened. "Oh. Your truck. My car."

"Yeah. How about if you take Emmet back to The Haven. I need to get to the ranch. I've got stuff to do." Not that he wanted to leave Olivia. But Gabe needed some time and distance from her to think about that kiss, about what it implied.

About where he wanted it to go. And where it couldn't.

"Sure. Thanks, Gabe." She pointed to her car. "Over here, Emmet."

"Thank you for helping me, Gabe," the little boy said.

"My pleasure. Feel better, okay?" Gabe smiled as the kid nodded.

Olivia shepherded Emmet into her car and ensured his seat belt was fastened before she opened her door. After a moment's thought she turned and called, "See you later?"

"I'll be there to pick up Eli, as usual." But man, Gabe wanted to go with her now, to sneak a few more moments holding her, kissing her again. His brain held him back.

Remember Eve, cowboy? Think carefully about what you're about to do, about where this could leave you.

"Then thanks again." Olivia gave him a big smile before she got into her car and drove away.

Gabe figured there were probably a hundred jobs

waiting for him back at the Double M, but he stood exactly where he was for several minutes, watching Olivia's car disappear.

He couldn't love Olivia. But he did. He wanted to be with her, listen to her dreams and fears, tell her about his own. He wanted to ask her opinion about his birthday party idea for Eli and make sure she'd be there for it.

He wanted her to stay. Forever.

But loving Olivia scared him. To be so dependent? To need someone as badly as he needed her in his world, to once again invest himself in love? What if it didn't work out? What if she couldn't or wouldn't stay? What if loving him wasn't what she wanted?

His phone chimed with a text from his boss. How long will you be?

On the way, Gabe texted back. Thrusting away all thoughts of Olivia and what they might share if she loved him, he drove back to the ranch and concentrated on work for the rest of the day. But Livvie was never far from his thoughts.

Olivia's one-on-one with Skylar produced several results. But the best one was that after apologizing to Emmet, the two became best friends. Emmet made Skylar face his feelings instead of brushing them off. And Skylar taught Emmet confidence.

Three days later, watching the two of them roasting marshmallows, Olivia knew she'd been right not to send the boy home. Her heart sang with joy at the changes God was working in *her* kids.

Funny how they'd become hers, each one special, unique and loved. She'd taken the aunts' advice and initiated these smaller-sized get-togethers, times to sit around a campfire and talk about what returning home would be like for them. Slowly their deepest fears emerged.

Olivia's heart ached as they discussed how scary it felt to be moved from a familiar place to a new one where no one understood anything about you. She could empathize with those who spoke of how hard it was to be the only one who felt they didn't belong. Their pain touched her deepest soul as she whispered a prayer for those who'd lost families or couldn't find the love they longed for. Most of all she prayed they'd experience a deepening of the faith in God they were just learning about. Sometimes kids begged her to let them stay. Those were the hardest times of all for Olivia.

"Everyone at The Haven loves you so much, kids," she said gently, forcing back tears as she studied the faces peering at her so trustingly. "That's why we wanted to make your vacation here special. But soon you'll be leaving because—" she paused, imprinting each face on her mind to pray for later "—vacations don't last forever."

"They do for you," Skylar yelled. Olivia had just learned that Skylar was in a horrible home situation where he was basically ignored. He needed attention, any kind of attention to acknowledge him. "You belong here."

"You're wrong, Skylar." Olivia smiled at his astonished look. "I came here for a visit before I start my new job in Edmonton. I'm just helping out until my foster sister Victoria gets better."

"You mean you were a foster kid, too?" Tyler and the rest of the group stared at her in disbelief.

Never once had Olivia felt comfortable sharing her

past. But tonight her heart went out to these kids. They thought they were alone in the world. They'd leave tomorrow and perhaps never return. This would be her last intimate interaction with them as a group, and she longed to send them away with hope, to show them they weren't alone.

She wanted them to know that she had gone through the same longing and survived. No, better than that. She'd flourished. Maybe if she let God's light shine on them, her fears would be healed. For good.

"I was a foster child," she said. A sense of peace filled her and somehow it was okay to admit the truth, to let out all the awful secrets that had bound her spirit for so long. "When I was just a few days old, I was left in a hospital with only my name pinned to my blanket. I never knew my parents. I don't know if I ever had a family."

"But you got to come here," Skylar pressed.

"I came to The Haven when I was twelve." Olivia gazed at their sweet faces. "But before that I lived in lots of different homes. Some bad things happened to me along the way. Maybe things have happened to you, too."

"You never told us this before," Skylar accused. Not all the hard edges had been softened from him, but at least now Olivia understood a little of where he was coming from.

"No," she admitted.

"Why not?" He glared at her.

"I don't like to talk about my past. It hurts." No going back now. "Foster kids learn how to do lots of things, don't we? We learn not to cause a fuss. Maybe then we'll get to stay. That didn't work for me."

No child moved. Eyes remained on her face, and oddly enough that gave Olivia the freedom she needed.

"I became really good at being the babysitter, the one in charge, the person my foster parents asked to help with everything and depended on. But then something bad happened."

"What did you do wrong?" a little girl named Esther asked.

"I don't know." For the first time in eons, Olivia let herself relive that awful inability to free her foster sibling. Was there something she'd forgotten to do, something she'd missed? Despair hovered like a blanket waiting to drop.

"Livvie didn't do anything wrong." Gabe's quiet voice came from behind her. He sat down on the tree stump beside her, cradling a sleeping Eli on his knee while his other hand clasped hers. "Sometimes things happen that aren't anyone's fault."

"But *you* get blamed." Skylar nodded, his face miserable. "I know about that."

Esther ignored him. "What happened, Livvie?"

"A fire." Olivia clung to Gabe's hand as a flood of memories cascaded into her brain. *Let me say it, Lord. If it will help even one of these children, I need to say it.* "I got out of the house, but I couldn't save my foster brother. He died."

"Where were his mom and dad?" Skylar demanded.

"I—I don't remember." She glanced at Gabe, surprised by a new thought. "I don't remember them being there."

"Did they go somewhere and leave you in charge?" he asked, squeezing her fingers as she searched the awful memories for an answer.

"I don't know. It was night and I wasn't old enough to babysit. I was just a kid. Like you guys." Olivia squeezed her eyes closed, framing that horrible time in her mind.

"The parents came after," she said, slightly bemused by this revelation. "They were angry. They asked me how I got out and he didn't."

Gabe met her stare while truth filtered through her brain. In that moment those parents had wished her dead, but not because she was bad or because she'd *let* him die. They were just bereft parents aching to have their beloved son back.

"It was grief talking, Olivia. Grief."

She nodded with new understanding. But she couldn't speak. Not yet.

Esther knelt and laid her head on Olivia's knees. "I wish I could take away the hurt like you sometimes take our hurts."

"Thank you, Esther." Olivia's heart overflowed with love for this dear child. For all of them. "Thank you for listening. God is still taking away my hurt. I'm learning that sometimes if we talk to other people about the bad things that have happened to us, that also helps heal our hurt. Does anyone want to talk?"

It was as if a dam broke. One by one, in hushed voices with halting sentences the children began to reveal bad things they'd experienced, feared and endured. As if sensing the preciousness of this moment, no one interrupted. Each child waited, listened and comforted. For Esther that was through touch. For Skylar that was by encouragement. For Emmet that was simply sitting next to the sufferer, being there.

Through it all, Gabe's hand held hers, an anchor in a storm of emotion Olivia had neither anticipated nor prepared for. All she could do was silently pray.

Complete darkness had fallen when the last child's

story died away. The group sat silent, contemplative and yet at peace, as if nothing could ever be so bad again.

"When you go home, and life seems too hard to bear, I want you to remember this evening," Olivia said into the tender silence. "I want you to remember that we are never, ever alone. We have a heavenly Father who loves us more than we can ever imagine. We can always talk to Him and He will always listen. He knows all the sad, hurt things about you, and He knows how to make it better."

If they were so precious to her, how much more so to God?

"I always kept my hurt and fear tied up inside. Don't do that. When you need to tell your story to someone, do it. Tell your foster parents, or your social worker or your teacher. If nobody else will listen, I'll always listen. You all know how to email The Haven?"

Nods all around.

"If no one will listen, email me," she told them. "I will listen. I promise."

"Olivia." Gabe's hand tightened, his tone full of warning.

But Olivia was tired of holding back.

"Thank you all for sharing. You've made this a wonderful evening I will never forget. Now it's time for bed."

Counsellors shepherded their groups to their cabins. Olivia heaved a sigh.

"That was amazing," she said, feeling lighter, freer than she had in years. She hugged Gabe, careful not to disturb Eli. "Thank you for sharing it with me."

"But—"

"Hi, Livvie." Eli's eyelashes fluttered up. A big smile stretched across his face. "I was having this dream about my mom—" Seeing Gabe's mouth tighten into a forbidding line, he froze.

"That's wonderful, sweetheart," she said cheerfully, ignoring Gabe's fierce expression. "We should always remember those we love in our dreams. You can tell me all about your dream sometime."

"We need to go home now. It's late." Gabe dropped her hand and rose, setting Eli on his feet, but offering no reason for his impromptu visit. "Good night."

"Eli, honey, can you go up to the house with Marina for a minute." Olivia waved over the senior counselor. "I need to talk to your dad about something."

"Okay." Eli peeked a second look at Gabe, then hurried toward Marina.

"What is it?" Gabe demanded brusquely.

"The other day—you said you loved me. Was it true?" Might as well get all honesty in the open tonight.

"I don't say things I don't mean."

As declarations went, that left something to be desired. But Olivia persisted.

"Do you love Eli, too?"

"Of course," Gabe was obviously irritated. "You know that. Why would you even ask?"

"Because you just hurt your son, the child you claim to love. He wanted to tell you about his dream of his dead mother and you cut him off."

"I didn't say anything," he sputtered.

"You didn't have to. Your expression was enough." Olivia hated doing this, but she had to. Facing the truth hurt but it was less costly than ignoring it. She feared that Gabe would pay dearly one of these days and she so wanted to prevent that. "I love you, too, Gabe. You're honest and generous and caring, all the things I always longed for when I thought about loving someone." When he would have embraced her, she held him off. "Problem is, I don't believe you truly love me."

"What? Why not?" He glared at her.

"My darling Gabe. When I think about loving you, it takes all the room in my heart. I know who you really are. There are no shadows, no memories of anyone else, no fears that you'll hurt me as I've been hurt before. There's only you, the man that I love with every part of my heart. Can you say the same?"

"I don't know what you mean." His blue-eyed gaze searched hers.

"You can't love me, Gabe, not the way I need. That's because there's not enough room in your heart for me. I come in second." Though tears rolled down her cheeks, she ignored them and laid her palm on his chest, trying to soften her words. "It's too crowded in here with the past and with anger and bitterness toward Eve. If we were together you'd constantly compare us. You'd always be afraid I was going to do what Eve did to you and you'd hold back to protect yourself." She paused, caressed his cheek. "That's not love, Gabe. That's fear and it's a horrible way to live."

This would end everything they'd shared, but now that Olivia had faced her past, she couldn't go into the future with anything less than complete honesty.

"The Bible says perfect love casts out fear. That's what I want, what I need, Gabe. Perfect love, for me, Olivia. Love that's not tainted by the past or anger or bitterness from someone else. I won't accept anything less." She stopped, suddenly aware that he hadn't said a word. *Lord?* "Perfect love is what Eli needs, too, Gabe. That's what he deserves. I believe it's what his mother gave him, no matter what you think of her."

She could see Gabe didn't like that. But she couldn't, wouldn't apologize.

"God has wonderful things planned for you and me and Eli. But you can't see it, Gabe. You're too busy looking back, reliving the pain and anger repeatedly. Please, if not for me, then do it for your son. Forgive and trust that God has something amazing planned for your future. I love you. Goodbye."

After one last, painful study of his beloved face, Olivia walked to The Haven. She put on her happy face, teased her sisters, laughed with the aunties and bade Eli a sweet good-night before his father silently shepherded him out.

But once in her room she couldn't stop her tears.

"It hurts, God, more than I ever thought possible. But I won't settle for less than your best. It's time for a new day, a new life, with You in charge. Help me?"

One more week and then she'd leave behind The Haven, and the man and boy who'd carved a special place deep in her heart, but the memories were carved inside forever.

Chapter Twelve

As the end of August approached, Gabe deliberately altered his times of visiting The Haven to mesh with times when Olivia was busy elsewhere. He figured that out thanks to her big scheduling chart on the office wall.

Avoiding her worked until Friday evening when he went to pick up Eli and read, "Last event for Olivia."

Gabe's heart took a nosedive when he perused her notes about tomorrow's treasure hunt hike for a group of ten-year-olds. He knew she'd been nervous about hosting it since the two brothers who were experienced counselors and would have accompanied her had left yesterday for a family emergency.

Gabe figured being responsible for seven young kids with two newbie counselors would test Olivia's determination to trust God, but he also knew there was no way she would cancel and disappoint the kids, especially given the aunts' oft-repeated insistence that each of their guests must experience the beauty of The Haven's wooded surroundings.

But the schedule wasn't the only source of Gabe's knowledge about the treasure hunt. For the past week

Eli had nagged incessantly about going along, insisting it was the only gift he wanted for his upcoming birthday. So far Gabe had refused, but today he'd learned The Haven's hired hand, Jake, would be accompanying Olivia. Jake had been working with the program since its inception. He had plenty of experience with the youth groups who visited and with The Haven's surroundings. He could be counted on to watch out for Eli. Today Gabe had promised Eli he'd ask Olivia's permission for his son to accompany her on the treasure hunt.

"Lose someone?" The object of his thoughts stood framed in the doorway. Olivia's voice was friendly as always. Her usual smile welcomed him. But there was a reticence in her silvery gray eyes he'd not seen before. "Eli's playing with Mikey on the climbing apparatus."

"I saw him, thanks." The thought of her leaving made Gabe's stomach clench. "I'm actually here to talk to you."

"Oh?" Olivia's glance didn't meet his. Instead, she walked to the desk, sat down behind it and folded her hands. "What can I do for you, Gabe?"

"Eli's been bugging me to go on your treasure hunt tomorrow. I know he's way younger than the others and I've told him no a hundred times, but he keeps saying that's the only thing he wants for his birthday, so I was wondering…" This wasn't as easy as he'd expected. Because of that invisible wall between them?

"Ah." Olivia chuckled. "He finally got to you." She grinned at his surprise. "He's been bugging me, too. I said he had to ask you."

"His birthday is next week—do you think he'd be okay? It wouldn't be too much?" The fatherhood business was filled with potholes of doubt that left Gabe uncertain about his decisions. He met Olivia's amused glance. "Say no if you think he can't handle it."

"Ordinarily I would. But as it happens, I had a call from the youth center in Edmonton. They're sending the kids we'd scheduled plus two eight-year-olds and one seven-year-old. Also, Mikey wants to join us, so I've modified the trip. Eli should be fine. Have him here at eight thirty please."

"He's not all that strong," Gabe fussed. "He says Jake is going. I can go, too, if—" Olivia's glare stopped him.

"If what? I can't manage." She arched one eyebrow. "We'll be fine, thanks."

"That wasn't—"

"After all this time, even though you claimed to love me, you still don't trust me." Her voice tight, Olivia pinned him with a look as he was about to backtrack. "I am not Eve, Gabe. I'm not going to break your heart and run away with your child," she said through gritted teeth.

"I never said—"

"You don't need to say it," she snapped. "It's evident in everything you do, in the way you act toward me and Eli. The past controls you. You cling to your unforgiveness and foresee so many problems that it blocks out the wonder of your son."

"I see Eli just fine." Gabe so did not want to go through this again, to hear her denunciation. "You cannot possibly know what it's like," he muttered.

"To know that a wonderful little boy has come into your world and that now you're not alone anymore? To be given the gift of fatherhood to a sensitive, artistic child who only wants to love and be loved?" Her ragged voice grabbed at his heart, reminding him of her comments about wanting to be a mother. "No, Gabe. I don't know what that's like. I wish I did."

"Olivia." He could hardly stand to hear the pain in her words, to see her wounded eyes. He stepped forward, wanting to comfort her, to make the hurt go away, but she held up a hand. The loss of the closeness they shared annoyed him, and he blurted out the first thing that came to mind. "He talks about her all the time as if she was perfect."

"Because to Eli, she was." Olivia shook her head. "Kids usually think of their mother that way. Didn't you?" She smiled as if reminded of her own childhood. "I had many foster mothers and they all had their faults. But some of them really tried to be my mother, to love and care for me. None more than Aunt Tillie and Aunt Margaret." Her chin thrust out. "What's wrong with loving someone because they loved you? The Bible says we love God because He first loved us."

Gabe couldn't object, not with all that passion and conviction in her voice. But she hadn't known Eve. His ex was nothing like the women she was describing. She'd been self-centered and grasping and—

"Why can't you shelve your view of Eve long enough to see how much your son loved his mother? I mean, who else did he have? His aunt Kathy?" Olivia was furious. Her voice oozed scorn. "Don't you get it? Who cares what you think of Eve? The fact is she adored that little boy, and he knew it. She left him a legacy of love. Whatever else she was, Eve was an amazing mother."

A bell rang somewhere on the grounds of The Haven. Gabe's jaw unclenched. It didn't matter that Eve had ruined his life? This woman didn't have a clue.

"That bell is for me, for my crafting class." Olivia

rose and walked past him to the door. There she paused, turned back and asked in a very solemn voice, "Sounds like you wanted perfection. Were you the perfect husband, Gabe? Are you positive you're the best father Eli could have? Will the legacy you leave him be something he'll cherish when you're gone?"

Her gaze held his for an interminable time. A thousand defenses rushed through his brain, but somehow Gabe knew Olivia would shoot down every one of them. And somewhere deep inside, he knew she was right. Eve had done well with Eli. Gabe needed to move on.

God knew he wanted to. If only...

Olivia walked out the door. It seemed to Gabe that all the joy and happiness he'd recently found in sharing his life with her left, too.

"It won't be an easy walk, Eli," Gabe warned early the next morning as he made sure his son's boots were securely tied. "You'll have to keep up with the others and do everything Olivia and Jake tell you to. No arguing."

"I know." Eli flung his arms around Gabe's neck and hugged as hard as he could. "Thank you," he whispered. "It's the bestest birthday present ever."

Better than anything your mom gave you?

Instantly ashamed, Gabe smoothed the unruly hair. They needed to fit in a haircut day before school started, he thought, startled by the rush of love that filled him.

Eli's first day of school.

How many more firsts would there be for them?

Would they all be without Olivia?

"Thank you very much." Even in this moment of gratefulness, Eli didn't say *Dad* or *Daddy*. Would he ever?

"You're welcome. But listen carefully now." Gabe lifted Eli onto one of the stools at the kitchen island and sat down beside him. "I know you're very strong and we've been practicing hiking. You've done well. You're an excellent hiker."

"Yep." Eli's grin revealed the tooth that had fallen out yesterday. "I am."

Gabe smiled while his mind searched for exactly the right way to phrase what he needed to say.

"I'm sure you'll enjoy yourself today. To celebrate, I have a gift for you. It's your own phone." He pulled a brand-new cell phone from his pocket. "We're going to put this in your backpack."

"Why?" Eli looked confused.

"Because that's what people do with their phones. They take them everywhere they go."

"Oh." Eli studied the item. "Why do I need it?"

"Well, let's say you get tired and don't want to keep going on the hike today. Maybe you want to quit because your boots hurt or because Mikey doesn't want to walk anymore. Here's what you do." He showed the boy how to press a button that immediately dialed his own cell phone.

"Your phone is ringing," Eli said, eyes wide.

"Your phone is calling mine." He ended the call and handed the new one to Eli. "Now you try it."

Eli's forehead pleated as he stabbed the key he'd been shown. Immediately Gabe's phone began to ring.

"Now what?" Eli asked blankly.

"Now you talk into it, to me. I'll go into the other room, okay?" Gabe walked to the bathroom, smiling at Eli's heavy breathing. "Are you there, son?" he asked when nothing was forthcoming.

"Yep. I can hear you," Eli shouted.

"Shh. Use your quiet voice now. Pretend you're in the woods and there are some lovely birds nearby. If you yell they'll fly away and you won't be able to take their picture or draw them."

"Oh." Eli waited. "Is this better?" he murmured.

"Perfect." Gabe returned to the kitchen. "So that's how it works."

"Cool." Eli studied the device with wonder. "Mikey hasn't got a phone."

"Well, this one is only for special occasions. Like today." He wanted to reinforce its intended use. "Do you remember what it's for?"

"Uh-huh. If don't wanna be on the treasure hunt no more then I phone you."

"And then what?" Gabe pressed.

"I dunno." Eli shrugged.

"Then I'll come and get you."

"In the woods?" Eli's blue eyes expanded.

"Wherever you are. Doesn't matter," Gabe assured him solemnly. "If you want to leave, you call me and I'll come get you. I'll always come if you ask me to, Eli," he emphasized. "Whenever you need me. Because you're my son and I love you very much."

"I love you, too." Eli initiated a second hug and Gabe hung on a little longer than strictly necessary. He was beginning to understand that he needed to cherish every one of these precious moments spent with his boy.

"Wait till Livvie sees my phone." Eli tucked it into a special pocket inside his backpack. "She'll be happy. Anyway, she's always happy."

"Um, maybe, just for today, we won't tell her about

your phone," Gabe murmured, irritated that he hadn't thought of this before.

"Why?" Eli's innocence grabbed at him.

Because she'll think I don't trust her. And phones were not allowed on her hikes. Eli would be breaking her rules.

"I think it would be better if you didn't tell her about the phone until after your hike is over." Seeing Eli's frown, Gabe quickly added, "We don't want her to think that you don't want to go on the hike," he said. "Or that you can't finish," he added.

"No, 'cause I'm a big boy." Eli's thin chest pushed outward. He nodded. "I know how to keep a secret," he said proudly.

"It's not exactly a secret—"

But Eli had already raced out of the house, yelling "C'mon," as he went.

Gabe followed. Was he too overprotective? Was he becoming one of those helicopter parents the news had talked about last night, trying to protect his kid from life?

"He's younger than the others," he mumbled as he grabbed his keys. "And he's never been on a real hike in the woods." And then as he headed for his truck, he added, "He's *my* kid."

As if that had exempted Eli from any of life's harsh realities.

At The Haven the treasure hunt group was assembling. Eli, backpack flopping, raced up to Olivia and hugged her leg.

"I'm here," he squealed.

"Really?" To Gabe's surprise she giggled as she bent

to pick him up and swung him around. "I hadn't noticed." Olivia usually didn't pick up the kids.

"Yes, you did," Eli laughed.

"Yes, I did. Did you bring everything on the list?" she asked as she glanced at Gabe.

"Yes. An' I brought—" Eli stopped, looked at Gabe, then shook his head once. "I got everything," he said.

"Good." She looked questioningly at Gabe. He shrugged as if to say, *Kids*.

After a moment she turned her attention to the group, introduced Jake and the two accompanying counselors while she laid out the guidelines. She then gave each person a small plastic zipper bag to store the items they would seek while on their treasure hunt. The same old rush of love sprang up inside him for this amazing woman.

If only—

"We'll leave in five minutes," she announced.

Gabe had hoped to ask her about his ideas for Eli's birthday party, but Olivia avoided him. Perhaps that was for the best. She'd be leaving soon. Once she was in Edmonton, the ties between them would be cut. He'd have to manage on his own.

Why did that feel so final, so horrible?

Gabe accepted Eli's goodbye hug, reminded him softly about the phone in his backpack and nodded at Eli's assurance that he wouldn't need it. Then he watched the group leave, singing a happy song as they went. He stood there watching until he couldn't see either Eli or Olivia anymore.

"Separation anxiety, dear?" Tillie threaded her arm through his. "Olivia's a fantastic director. She'll take care of Eli, don't you worry."

"Yes, she will." On his other side, Margaret sighed. "I wish she could stay. It's been so wonderful to have her logical brain smoothing out all the issues that snarl things up."

"Then what would Victoria do?" Gabe asked, reminding them of their other foster daughter.

"Oh, my dear. There's so much to do. Victoria would be over the moon if Livvie stayed. She'd like to share the job, leave the office running to Livvie." Tillie's voice died away.

"But Olivia wants to go to her job in Edmonton," he guessed.

"You know, I don't believe she does." Margaret shook her head. "I believe she's found her confidence here. That's why she can take that group today. Her fear is gone. She's trusting God to meet her needs and direct her. She's grown so much."

"We've been praying for our Livvie to let go of the past and allow the love she keeps bottled inside to spill out." Tillie smiled at him. "Isn't it wonderful to see it happening? Especially with your little Eli. My, she does love that child."

"I think leaving him behind will be hardest of all for her. And you, of course." Margaret smiled. "You're fond of her, too, aren't you, Gabe?"

"Yes, I am." What was the point of denying the truth? Gabe swallowed. Though "fond" hardly seemed strong enough for what he felt. "I love Olivia."

"But there's a problem." Tillie nodded. "I've seen it."

"We both have," Margaret agreed. "And from what little our dear girl has confided, we think it has to do with your past. Is there anything we can do to help you?"

Gabe was fed up with feeling like he'd done something wrong. His anger at Eve wasn't wrong. It was well deserved. But here was his chance to get some more advice and he wasn't about to waste it.

"I talked to you about forgiveness before and you suggested some things, but, well, they don't work. I can't forgive my ex-wife."

"Oh, my dear boy." Tillie laid her head on his shoulder. "You must."

"Why?" he demanded. "She doesn't deserve it. She lied, cheated, stole Eli's childhood. Because of her I've missed all the milestones in my son's life," he blurted, desperate for a sympathetic ear that would understand his battle.

"My dear man. Forgiving isn't about her," Tillie said with a shake of her head. "It's about you. It's about freeing yourself from that burden."

"Besides, it's because of your wife that you have a son," Margaret said, her tone just the tiniest bit severe. "A boy whose mother made certain he knew he was loved. Do you understand what a legacy that is to a child, Gabe? Do you understand how many children never receive such love?"

They didn't understand his position, either.

"Olivia says it doesn't matter what I feel about Eve," he snapped.

"No, it really doesn't. God says forgive. You don't get to pick who." Margaret looked quite severe.

"The thing you must keep foremost, my dear, is to balance what you gain by forgiveness against what you lose." Tillie shrugged. "It's really no contest."

"But forgiving Eve means she gets off scot-free."

"And not forgiving her means you're punishing her?"

Margaret raised her eyebrows. "She's beyond your reach, dear. You're only punishing yourself."

Frustrated, irritated and feeling alone in his misery, Gabe made an excuse and went home. Of all the days off he'd longed for, this wasn't one he wanted. He cleaned the house, did the laundry and made a popcorn dessert his dad used to make for him. It was one Eli loved.

But thoughts of Olivia filled every moment. In Eli's room he dusted the treasure box she'd made him from an old shoebox covered with gold foil and decorated with stars. Gabe unloaded the dishwasher and stared at the big white platter she'd given him as a housewarming gift because she'd said he'd need it for his Thanksgiving turkey. He watered the tubs of cascading red petunias she'd helped Eli choose and plant.

Chores completed, Gabe sat in his living room with a steaming cup of coffee, trying to come up with something else to keep busy. That's when it hit him. He was alone and that's how it was going to be from now on. Eli would grow up, play with his friends, make a whole world for himself. And Gabe would be alone because Olivia was leaving.

He'd have nobody to talk things over with, to help make decisions, to laugh with at Eli's goofiness. No one to encourage Gabe with a salty comment or a challenge. No one to press him on whether he'd based his decision biblically.

Loneliness swamped Gabe as he realized that Olivia was rooted inside him. Whether she was present or not, the aunts' organized foster daughter now filled every niche and corner of his world. The artwork he'd chosen at Chokecherry Hollow's local fair reminded him of her smile. The stove reminded him of her laughter when he'd burned an expensive roast in it. His mind repeated the prayer he'd overheard the day he'd moved in. She'd thought she was alone and had asked God to bless him and Eli as they became a family.

How could they be a family without her?

Olivia was a necessary part of Gabe's world. Avoiding her this past week had proved just how integral she'd become to his life. He thought about her when he made coffee exactly as she'd shown him. He thought about her when he was making dinner, whether she'd approve of his meal plan, and if she'd approve of the new school clothes he'd bought for Eli. It was Olivia who'd made this home a reality for him and Eli.

But mostly Gabe thought about what she'd said, how she'd dissed his claim of love.

There's not enough room in your heart for me. It's crowded with the past and with hate for the woman who left you. I think you'd always be afraid I was going to do what Eve did. That's not love, Gabe.

If only he could shed this unyielding chunk of bitterness inside, but even the aunts couldn't help him with that.

Chapter Thirteen

Olivia was ecstatic. The treasure hunt hike was going so well. Of course, it hadn't been without its issues, but she'd handled them with Jake and the newbie counselors' help. Her pleasure grew as the kids laughed with each discovery. She was thrilled to hear their giggles when they took time to shed their shoes and socks and dip their toes in the cool creek. It felt so good to share these moments without worrying.

"I know we had lunch, guys, but it's so warm I think we need another break. Let's share a snack. Then you can lay out all the items you've collected so we can make sure everyone has one of each. After all, we need every single item on our lists if we're going to get that treasure."

"You've done an amazing job here," Jake praised as the kids finished off their juice boxes and the cereal treats she'd brought. "There's a big variance in age in this group, yet you've managed to make it fun for all of them."

"It's nothing," she demurred breezily. But Jake wasn't buying.

"Yes, it is, Olivia. You relate to every kid. You make each one feel appreciated and that gives them a sense of accomplishment. You've done an excellent job for The Haven." He crushed his box and put it in the trash bag they'd brought. "You have a lot to offer your aunts' ministry. Why not stay?"

Olivia noticed Eli had curled up on his backpack and was now sleeping. So were three of the other younger children. The rest of the group seemed content to quietly discuss their treasures, comparing them and musing about what the final treasure might be.

"There won't be anything for me to do when Victoria returns," she murmured.

"But you wish you *could* stay?" Jake pressed, then nodded. "This place does that to you. You think that you're only here for a little while and you end up staying."

"That's what happened to you?" Her curiosity rose. Jake was such a major part of The Haven that it was hard to remember he hadn't always been here. The aunts had never explained why Jake had come or why he'd stayed, and Olivia had never asked.

"I was just going to help out for a while, to pay the aunts for caring for me." He shrugged. "I guess it's never seemed like quite the right time for me to leave."

"It never will be," she said, aghast at the thought of Jake leaving. "This is your home."

"It's yours, too," he said quietly.

"Yes." She shrugged. "I've struggled to forget my past. I always thought leaving here, getting as far away as I could, was the answer. But being here, the responsibility of having to take over this ministry while Vic gets better—that's what has helped me deal with the dragons in my past and learn to depend on God."

"That's The Haven effect. And your aunts'." He twiddled with a thread on his shirt. "Somehow they seem to just know what each of us needs."

"They'd tell you that's the God effect," Olivia said with a chuckle.

"Will it be hard for you to leave? Especially Gabe and Eli?" he asked soberly.

"Very."

"He loves you," Jake said quietly.

"But not enough," she returned sadly. "I'm trying to trust that God has a plan for my life. I guess Gabe and Eli aren't part of it." She checked her watch.

"Yeah, time to go." Jake pulled a bit of straw and stuck the stem between his teeth. "Sometimes it takes a lot to knock sense into the heads of stubborn cowboys," he mused in a twang straight from Texas, then smiled at her.

"Well said. I—"

A noise from the shrubs ahead of them made Olivia freeze. She recognized that sound. Jake did, too.

"Stay put," he whispered. "Tell the kids to do the same while I check it out." He unzipped his pack to show her the butt of his rifle.

"But a black bear—" she began, but Jake read her thoughts.

"I know. The law says I can only shoot if it attacks us. If we don't do anything threatening, I doubt it will. But I'll have a better idea what we're dealing with when I get a look," he finished. "Call the wildlife authorities and explain our situation."

"Okay. Be careful, Jake."

"Pray," he murmured, then crept away, his steps almost soundless in the green underbrush.

Olivia quickly made the call, grimacing when she was told the officers were attending to another call and might take a while to arrive. As quietly as possible she gathered the children around her, heart thudding as she wakened Eli and cuddled him close.

She was the one responsible here. With her Father's help, she was not letting one of them be hurt. *Please, God, help us.*

A moment later Jake returned. His tight face said all she needed to know.

"A mom and her cub. They're right in the middle of our path, feasting on the berries. We can't back up or go around so we're going to have to wait it out."

"Okay. Thanks." She quietly addressed the children. "I need you to pay close attention. There is a mother bear nearby with her baby. They're eating berries to fill up before they have their long sleep all winter." The children's eyes grew huge.

"What do we do?" one of them asked, voice panicky.

"Will that bear eat us?" Eli asked.

"No. This is a mommy bear with her baby. She isn't interested in us. She just wants her baby to eat his berries so he'll be able to sleep during the winter. If we're quiet and leave her alone, she doesn't care about us. She only wants the food," she emphasized.

Jake stepped away to the edge of the clearing. He peered into the forest. Olivia knew he was monitoring every moment of the bear and her cub. Because *she* was watching him, the kids were watching him. She could feel their fear mounting.

"The first thing we're going to do is ask God to help us," she told them, and then began praying. Several children added their own prayers. When silence fell, she lifted her head and smiled. "God has heard us. We can depend on Him to help us. Now, I'm going to tell you some of the things I know about bears while we wait for the people I've called to come and help us. But you must remember to be very quiet. We don't want to scare the mother."

Olivia told them story after story, everything she'd read about the Rockies wildlife, studied in school, learned from the aunties and later from Jake. As she did she thought of Gabe, trusting her to watch the son he'd only just begun to know. Her heart sent up another plea for help when she remembered how she'd chided him for doubting she could handle this treasure hunt. Why hadn't she asked him to come along instead of attacking him?

Please, God, help us. Please send someone.

"They're coming closer," a little girl whispered.

"It's going to be dark soon," one of the eldest kids noticed.

We need to get out of here, God!

"We'll be fine." Olivia met Jake's glance. She tried to place a second call to the wildlife service and found her cell phone was dead, despite the new battery she'd installed and fully charged since her new phone hadn't yet arrived. Jake had no cell phone, but he had a walkie-talkie to reach The Haven, but it made a lot of noise and he was hesitant lest it startle the bears.

Lord, I'm trusting You to keep these children safe. Please help us. I'm the responsible one. I suggested this treasure hunt as a way for the younger kids to participate in The Haven's program. Don't let me be the cause of this ministry failing, of children getting hurt. I'm trusting in You to deliver us.

The words spilled from Olivia's heart in a steady stream until a very soft, very plaintive voice penetrated her consciousness.

"Daddy? There's a bear. Can you help?"

Olivia blinked. Eli held a tiny cell phone. Two things hit her at the same time.

Daddy. He said "Daddy".

He's asking Gabe to help us.

Olivia's heart swelled with praise. Two answers to prayer.

"Sweetie, let me—" She froze when Eli clenched the phone tight to his ear, listened and then nodded his head.

"Okay, Daddy. I'll do it. Then can you come and get me?" the plaintive request came. "I want to go home." Another nod, then Eli handed her the phone.

"Gabe?"

"Tell me where you are, Olivia. Exactly." His gruff voice made her heart swell. She trusted him, knew he'd save his son. Gabe loved Eli.

"There's a little map on the wall in my office. Just follow it." She recited the landmarks they'd passed, the small glen and the path they'd taken to get here.

"You know the rules," he said, sounding angry. "Stay quiet, in one place and together. And wait. I'll get there as quickly as I can."

"What am I waiting for?" she asked, confused.

"You'll know," Gabe said.

She wanted to thank him, to tell him she loved him, that she needed him in her life forever.

But Gabe had hung up.

"Olivia." Jake's urgent whisper got her attention.

She twisted, saw the mother bear lurch to her hind feet and sway for a moment before her eyes fixed on Olivia's little group.

"Oh, Lord—help!"

* * *

Stark fear overtook Gabe as he grabbed his truck keys and drove to The Haven. He took the map, had a short conversation with Victoria, then climbed on a quad and set off on the path Olivia had charted for the treasure hunt. Heart in his throat, he drove quickly, offering desperate prayers for the little group's safety.

For as long as he lived he would never forget Eli's scared voice calling him Daddy. How sweet that sound. Yet how terrorizing to hear his son beg him for help. No way was he going to disappoint his child.

Branches slapped Gabe in the face as he drove. The sting against his cheeks, the damp of a light rain trickling down his neck and the discomfort of jarring over the trail barely registered as truth began to dawn inside his hardened heart.

Olivia was right. The past didn't matter. Eve, her deceit, all the wrong she'd done him—they were immaterial now. Gabe could lose the future with his son, could lose the woman he cared for more than his own life. He'd gladly be hurt a hundred times over if it would protect Eli or Olivia. Nothing mattered as much as they did.

So what if loving Olivia broke his heart? Wasn't that better than never loving her? And anyway, who said he'd get hurt. Olivia didn't hurt those she cared about. She protected them. She would gladly lay down her own life if it would save any one of those children she was with.

That couldn't happen!

Gabe couldn't lose her or Eli, not now, not when he'd finally realized the past didn't matter. God had gifted him with two special loves, a future, a chance to watch his boy grow up, to teach him about God and love. A chance to love Olivia and be loved. Was he going to lose his chance to grab happiness because he couldn't let go of the past?

"You're a fool, Webber," he muttered, jaw clenched in determination.

Olivia was going to leave because he hadn't told her that nothing mattered more than her, that she would always be the most important person in his world. Could he stand back and let her go? Could he live each day without remembering the memories they'd made, thinking of new ones they could make? No! But he'd messed up so badly. Would she forgive him, take a chance on him? Was there a way to make it up to Olivia and Eli?

Love them.

Gabe smiled at the voice in his head. Love was always the answer. How silly to forget that.

"Hang on, Eli. Hang on to Olivia. I'll be there soon." It was slow going now. The quad didn't fit on the walking path, which meant he sometimes had to ride leaning to one side. But Gabe wouldn't even consider giving up on his beloved ones.

"Forgive me for being so stupid, Lord," he prayed as he traveled. "You are love and forgiveness. I lost sight of that for far too long."

As Gabe asked for forgiveness, the rock-solid nugget that had lain in his heart since Eve's departure from his life began to melt and dissolve until he felt only freedom and joy. Okay, and a little fear.

"But I'm trusting You," he said out loud to conquer it, and then he quoted, "'What time I am afraid, I will trust in Thee.'"

The rain fell harder, soaking him. But Gabe didn't feel it because he was on a mission.

A mission of love.

* * *

Olivia wanted to grab the kids and hug them as close as she could. But she knew moving now was the wrong thing to do, so she fixed her gaze on the bear and maintained eye contact.

Clearly agitated at finding them so near her feeding spot, the mother bear growled menacingly. From the corner of her eyes, Olivia saw Jake take aim.

"Please help us, God. She's just a mom protecting her baby. I'm trusting You."

The bear sank onto all fours. She was going to charge. Olivia held her breath.

A shrill whistle pieced the afternoon. Once, twice, three times. The mother bear jerked her head from side to side, trying to locate the sound.

"Again, Eli," she heard Jake say. And Eli blew twice more. "Get out of here, bear," Jake yelled. "Everyone, stand up as tall as you can and yell really loud."

Each child did as they were asked. Confused and obviously concerned about her cub, the mother grunted loudly, then swung her head to one side. After surveying them a moment longer, she nudged her cub and together they lumbered off into the woods.

The entire group burst out cheering.

"I'll make sure she's gone," Jake murmured. "Stay here."

Olivia nodded. She felt wilted, as if her knees were jelly. "Thank You, God," she whispered. A few minutes later Jake returned. "Gone?"

"Yes. The wildlife guys will have to catch her and her cub and move them outside the fence. Then we'll need to get that fence inspected. We can't have that happening again." He heaved a sigh. "Let's get back to The Haven. I could use a big mug of your sister's strongest coffee."

"Me, too. How did you know to bring your rifle?" she asked.

"I was out riding last night and thinking about this path and decided I'd bring it just in case. Didn't want to alarm anyone. I should have run the perimeter before we left." He wore a grim expression. "I won't make that mistake again."

"You always look after everyone at The Haven so well." Olivia smiled. "The aunties are blessed to have you. Thank you, Jake."

"My pleasure." With his rifle tucked away in his bag, he began encouraging the kids to pick up any trash they'd dropped.

"Did I blow it okay? Daddy said to be real loud." Eli studied his whistle.

"Honey, you were amazing. I didn't know you had a whistle," she said, smoothing his hair with a trembling hand. *Or a cell phone.*

"I din't know neither," Eli said with a grin. "Daddy said he put it in in my backpack in case I got losted, so you could find me in the woods. But I didn't get losted." He stopped, listened and then grinned so wide Olivia couldn't help but smile in return. "He's coming! Do you hear? He's coming just like he said he would."

"Of course. Your daddy will always come if you ask him, Eli. He loves you very much." Eli wasn't the only one who'd learned a lesson today. Olivia had learned she could trust Him in every situation. Always. Even when she had to leave here and move on.

At that moment Gabe barreled through the brush and stopped in the middle of their resting spot.

"Daddy!" Eli raced to his father and laughed with glee when Gabe jumped off the quad and swung him into his arms. "I blowed the whistle just like you said, Daddy, and the bear runned away."

"Good man." Gabe pressed his lips against the dark hair so like his own, then gazed into his child's face. "You scared me, Eli."

"Why?" Eli rubbed a hand against his dad's bristly jaw, reveling in the experience.

"Because I love you very much. I don't ever want anything bad to happen to you."

"But nothin' did 'cause Livvie prayed and I blowed the whistle an' Jake said God sent the bear away." Eli hugged his father, then leaned away and said very gently, "I love you, too, Daddy. I won't talk about Mommy no more 'cause it hurts you an' Livvie says we shouldn't do stuff to make other people sad."

"Oh, Eli." Olivia was pretty sure those were tears in Gabe's eyes, though he quickly ducked his head into his son's neck. "You can talk about your mom whenever you want," he said, his voice very quiet. "I want you to tell me all about her. I'd like to know about such a wonderful mom like yours."

"Really?" Eli asked, then grinned when Gabe nodded. "Well, she always smelled really nice." He sniffed, then wrinkled his nose, obviously not getting the same vibe from Gabe.

Olivia smothered a chuckle as the boy wiggled to be free. Gabe set Eli down, one hand resting on his shoulder as if he couldn't quite let go. Her aching heart eased a little at the sight of Gabe's fierce love.

"Can I ride home on that bike with you, Daddy?"

"If Olivia says it's okay." Gabe's eyes met hers, but

she couldn't read the expression in them. "Are *you* all right?" he asked very quietly, his gaze intense.

"Yes. God took care of us." She smiled. "But thank you for the whistle."

"Hey, Gabe." Jake slapped him on the shoulder. "The wildlife people are probably using that old road to the west to get here. Can you go back that way and tell them to head toward Flinder's Crossing? I tracked that mother and her cub in that direction."

"Sure," Gabe agreed, but his gaze remained on her.

"We'd better head back, too," Jake said, glancing from him to Olivia. "Before daylight's completely gone. At least the drizzle has stopped."

"Yes. Let's go." She smiled at Eli. "See you back at The Haven," she said, meeting Gabe's solemn gaze.

"You will."

There was something different about him, she decided as she herded the little group toward home. Something softer?

"Probably worry about his son," she told herself and focused on helping Mikey, who wouldn't go with Eli, navigate the rougher spots. "You're in charge now, so do your job and stop mooning over something you can't have."

"Are you talkin' to me, Aunt Livvie?" Mikey frowned. "'Cause I don't know what mooning means."

"Nor should you, Mikey, my boy. Let's see who can go up this hill the fastest?" She smiled as he dashed upward. Kids were so precious. Kids and families. That's what made life worthwhile.

And tall lean cowboys who didn't smile much and yet still managed to say a thousand things with their intense blue eyes. If only...

Chapter Fourteen

Back at The Haven, a very frustrated Gabe stayed for supper and endured the children's repeated accounts of their treasure hunt as he waited for an opportunity to talk to Olivia. But the woman seemed intent on avoiding him.

"Hey!" Mikey's frown expressed his dissatisfaction. "We never got no treasure!"

Victoria tried to suggest they needed rest and could get it in the morning, but that didn't fly. Every child in the room began demanding to see the "treasure." Gabe fully expected Olivia to agree and lead them to it; instead, she beckoned to him to follow her outside.

"What's wrong?" he asked, surprised by the deep, dark flush covering her face.

"The treasure. The stupid treasure," she muttered. When he simply stared at her, she snapped in exasperation, "I forgot to bury it."

Gabe couldn't help it. He burst out laughing. It was such an anticlimactic event and the opposite of Ms. Organization's usual style that he took a moment to simply enjoy her discomfiture.

"Well? Are you going to help me or not?" she demanded grumpily as she slapped her hands on her hips in annoyance.

"Sure." He shrugged, loving the way her gray eyes turned silver and shot sparks of lightning when she was displeased. "What do you need me to do?"

"Tell them we can find it in the morning?" she begged, arching her neck.

"Too late for that, Olivia." Gabe inclined his head toward the kitchen where a chant of "treasure, treasure" emanated through the open windows.

"I didn't think it would work." She was tired. Who wouldn't be after such an experience?

Gabe's heart softened as he gazed at her. He would do this and anything else she asked of him, anytime, anywhere. He loved this woman so much and he was going to tell her so, only not now when a bunch of kids were yelling, demanding her attention. He was going to tell her when nothing and no one would interrupt.

"Just tell me what you need me to do," Gabe said tenderly.

"There's a wooden box in my office, under the red pillows. In it there are several bags of those little chocolate coins wrapped in gold foil and some small toys. You need to dig a hole and put our treasure chest in it."

"Okay." *I'd do anything for you, my darling.*

"That's not all, Gabe. The box has to be buried on the north side of the pottery shed because that's where the instructions will lead them." Olivia brushed pine needles off her sweater with a disgusted look. "Dig underneath that great big poplar tree. Oh. But before you bury the box, you need to tie a belt around it."

"A belt?" He blinked.

"Yes. It's part of the rhyme I wrote, but then I

couldn't find a belt, and then it was too late to rewrite the rhyme and we had to leave and that's why I didn't get around to burying the treasure. I thought I could do it while they ate, but…"

Gabe figured his face must have shown his confusion because Olivia exhaled in a long-suffering sigh before resuming her explanation.

"Their clues specifically say they have to unbuckle the chest and open it to find their treasure."

"Ah." He nodded. "So where do I find a belt?"

"I don't know. Improvise." The noise from the kitchen was deafening. Olivia looked like her last nerve was in danger of fraying. "I'll go keep them busy, but it won't be easy. Please, Gabe, don't take too long." She hurried away.

"Find the chest and a belt and dig a hole." The chest was easy to locate, and the stuff was inside just as she said. That's when Gabe had the idea. But by the time he'd completed his secret task, the noise was deafening, and he still didn't have a belt. He caught a glimpse of himself in the office mirror.

Really? You're willing to do that? his brain demanded.

Yep. Truth was, he'd do almost anything for Olivia.

Gabe lugged the box to the spot she'd mentioned, ran back for a shovel, found a soft spot and started digging. Ten minutes later the hole waited. He undid his belt, fastened it around the box and lowered it into the earth. He felt funny without the familiar weight around his waist but he backfilled the hole anyway. There were clumps of weeds nearby. He pulled a bunch up and replanted them under the tree. Then he smoothed the area. Hopefully the kids wouldn't notice the disturbance he'd made.

Then he hurried back toward the house, losing the

shovel on the way. Olivia and Jake were struggling to engage the kids in a game, but the response was lack-luster. Olivia lifted her head as he entered, a question mark in her lovely silver-gray eyes. For a moment Gabe stood transfixed, staring as he imagined all the futures they could have together. *If* she'd agree.

"Gabe?"

He swallowed hard before nodding.

"All right, children. You may now open your last clue." Olivia moved toward him as the sound of rustling paper filled the room. "Ideas? Anyone?"

"'Birds love my open arms,'" the eldest read, face screwed up in thought. "Nests?"

"Birdhouses?" another suggested.

The kids looked at each other, uncertainly.

"Trees." Eli smiled. "Birds like trees. That's where they build their nests."

"He's right. What's the next part of it?" one child said.

"'Kids like my shade for lunch.'" Again the eldest child spoke. He looked at Eli.

"Which tree?"

Gabe watched Olivia's face, saw the love in her eyes as her glance slid from one child to the next. She was perfect for this job. His heart grew impatient, but he wasn't going to rush things. He tilted back on the heels of his boots, waiting, praying, trying anything to chase away his doubts about his impetuous actions.

"We had our sandwiches under a tree," Eli murmured, brow wrinkled in thought. His eyes searched for and found Olivia. "You brought me lemonade when mine got spilled."

Olivia smiled and nodded. Then her glance swerved to Gabe. There was something unspoken there, something he wanted to know more about—when they were alone together.

"Good thing you came along, Eli," one of the kids cheered. "We wouldn't know where to look. Show us, Eli."

His chest proudly thrust forward, Eli led the way out the door and toward the pottery shed, the other kids following.

"Where's your belt, Gabe?" Olivia's voice came from just below his left shoulder, soft, filled with—affection?

"It was needed for a higher purpose." He so badly wanted to kiss her, to speak from his heart. But he wanted more than that for her. He wanted to make this so special she'd never forget. "You'd better join them," he said, letting her beauty soak into him. "This is your treasure hunt."

"And yours. Thank you, Gabe." She smiled and it was like fireworks went off. Then she joined the children, who were now pawing at the freshly dug earth.

Content to watch, Gabe held back, unable to stop smiling. Moments later there was a shriek of excitement as the box was unearthed.

"There's the belt, just like it said."

"Open it. I want to see what's inside."

He waited, almost breathless as the box was opened and the treasure distributed.

"Hey, this says Livvie's name." Eli held up a white envelope.

Olivia turned to look at Gabe, a question in her eyes. He simply watched her, saw the way she hesitantly took the note, slid her thumb under the seal and pulled out the slip of paper. She read it, then looked at him, eyes wide. With hope?

If only she still loved him.

The next few minutes passed in a blur for Gabe. Someone—Victoria?—urged the children to save their treasure for tomorrow and sent them scurrying for bed, insisting Eli and Mikey needed a sleepover. Gabe let his gaze slide off Olivia just long enough to embrace his son and kiss him good-night. He thought it was Jake who filled in the hole he'd dug, but then he, too, disappeared, leaving Gabe and Olivia alone on the tiny hill just above the house with the full moon shining on them.

"What does this mean?" she asked, holding up the note.

"Exactly what it says." Gabe took a step toward her, loving the fragrance of her hair on the night breeze. "You're my treasure. I love you."

"But—" A furrow appeared on her forehead.

"I'm free, Livvie. I've forgiven Eve, if there was ever anything to forgive." He took her hands in his just to make sure she heard him out and didn't run off before he'd said everything he needed to say. "When you and Eli were out there with a black bear—let's just say I got my priorities straight."

"And they are?" She wasn't quite sure of him. Not yet.

"That you and Eli are what matter most in my life. My marriage failed, but it wasn't all Eve's fault. It was mine, too. Given my heartless dismissal of her, it's no wonder she didn't tell me about Eli." He paused, stared into her eyes, loving the clarity he saw there. "But whose fault it was doesn't matter anymore. It's in the past. I'm more interested in the future."

"Which is?" Something in those silvery eyes warned Gabe to be very clear.

"I love you. I want to be with you. Always. And I don't care where that is." He inhaled silently, praying for the right words. "If you still want to live in Edmonton, I'll move there."

"But your new house—?"

"I don't want to be there if you won't share it," he said firmly.

"Your job, the horses, Eli's school?" He knew Olivia was listing them because she still wasn't certain about him. That was okay. If she loved him they would have the future for him to prove his love.

"There are lots of jobs, lots of horses, lots of schools," he said with a smile. "But there's only one you. You're the one I want in my life. You moved into my heart, Olivia, and now you own it. Wherever you go, Eli and I go. I love you."

"But—" She frowned as tears welled.

Gabe lifted one hand and gently smoothed a thumb under each eye, pushing away the tears.

"Darling Olivia, I have finally gotten my priorities straight and they are you. I love you, though I'm surely not good enough for you. I'll make mistakes and hurt you and not be half the man you deserve. I'm grumpy and selfish and disorganized and I've lost my belt which cowboys never do—"

"And you love me?" she added with a beatific smile. He nodded.

"I can't fathom why God would batter down my wall of bitterness, why He would take the time to make a dumbbell like me see how wrong I've been. And I'm so, so sorry that He had to use you and Eli to make me see sense. When I think of what could have happened—"

"God was in control, Gabe. We were in His hands." Her arms crept around his neck. "There is no better place."

"No." He liked the way she traced the curls at his

nape and touched the tips of his ears and the corners of his eyes. But he needed more. "Olivia?"

"I love you, Gabe. I want us to have a future together, too. You and Eli and me. A family. It's what I've always wanted, even when I didn't know it. But God knew. It's been hard to learn to trust Him completely, but knowing you love me is so very worth it—"

"Olivia, please." Gabe caught his breath at her beauty as she tipped her head back to stare at him. "Can I kiss you now?" he asked.

"I've been waiting and waiting," she whispered.

Olivia stood on her tiptoes and Gabe met her halfway, his lips touching hers with a promise that came from the depths of his soul. Without using a single word he told her that she was his beloved, the most important thing in his world.

"You don't need to worry, Olivia. You are and will always be first in my heart," he whispered when at last they drew apart. She smiled and nestled her head against his chest.

"And you'll always be my cowboy knight in shining armor, minus his belt," she teased with a giggle. Then she gazed at him, her silver eyes memorizing each angle of his face. "You're always there for me, Gabe, from the first day I came home. You've helped me realize that here at The Haven is where I belong."

"Just to be clear—you don't want to move to Edmonton?" he asked hesitantly.

"No," she whispered, her smile wide. "I want to be part of this amazing ministry. I want to trust God to show us how to help kids. I want to be here, so I can see their transformations. I want to be with you, Gabe, for as long as He gives us together, with Eli. I love you. If you love me, I have all I need."

He traced a fingertip over her lips, stunned by what God had worked out in his life. He didn't deserve it, but he was going to grab it and squeeze out every precious second of the time God gave him with this amazing woman.

"When can we get married, Olivia?" For the first time, when he cupped her face in his hands, his fingers tracing the scar in a gentle touch, Olivia didn't move.

"Well, you haven't actually asked me yet, Gabe," she giggled.

He immediately went down on one knee. He was dumb but not that dumb. When God gave you something wonderful, you hung on to it.

"My darling Olivia, I love you more than you will ever know. I want to marry you and share our wonderful future together. So, will you?"

Her fingers smoothed across his face, memorizing each detail as she studied him. For a moment Gabe's heart quaked, but then he remembered in whom he trusted and waited. At last a smile flickered across Olivia's face.

"Yes," she said, head tilted to one side. "I'm thinking October. Any objections?"

"Not a one," Gabe said as he rose and embraced her. "Fortunately, I already have a place for us to live."

"A very nice place," she agreed. "And a son we can love and raise to trust in God. Thank you, Gabe." She kissed him. "Suddenly I'm not tired at all."

"Me, neither. Let's sit here for a while and watch the stars."

So they did.

Chapter Fifteen

Gabe and Olivia chose to be married on Thanksgiving Monday at The Haven. Both the bride and groom wanted a simple family-centered event, outside if possible, in the splendor of the autumn-toned woods.

Overwhelmed with her new job as codirector of The Haven's outreach program, Olivia had only one weekend to shop for a wedding dress, but thanks to her aunties' preparation, that was more than enough to choose a beautiful shantung suit in purest ivory with matching heels.

The aunties also located the most perfect bridesmaid dresses with swirly chiffon skirts featuring Olivia's signature orange tones among multi hues of autumn greens, grays and browns. Once the dresses were chosen, Tillie and Margaret ordered gorgeous russet mohair yarn and hand-crocheted shrugs for each sister to provide a bit of extra warmth if the day turned chilly.

But, of course, it wasn't. Monday dawned a glorious day with a warmly glowing sun that turned the hills into a splendorous setting, certainly a day for Thanksgiving.

As Olivia waited for ring bearer Eli to finish his walk down the aisle to his father, she thought about how full her life was. The aunts, her sisters, their children, the youth who came to The Haven, and now Gabe and Eli.

Trust God? Always. He had given her the desires of her heart.

"Are you ready, dear?" Aunt Tillie's arm slipped through hers on the left, Aunt Margaret's on the right.

"Ready, aunties." Her gaze riveted on Gabe's face, Olivia walked down the aisle, certain that whatever their future brought, she could trust her Lord.

The couple repeated the vows they'd chosen with friends and family as witnesses and God's spectacular creation in the background. Olivia was lost in her first kiss as Gabe's wife when she felt someone tugging on her skirt.

"Congratulations," Eli said with careful enunciation.

"Thank you, darling." She bent and hugged him, hid a smile as the little boy shook his head. "Is everything okay, Eli?" she asked when his blue eyes, so like Gabe's, locked with hers.

"Yeah. I was just wondering. Are you my mommy now?"

Olivia felt Gabe's fingers tighten against her waist. She stood on tiptoe and kissed his cheek for reassurance before bending to address Eli.

"You had a wonderful mommy, Eli. I wouldn't ever try to take her place." She brushed her fingers against his cheek. "I'm just Olivia, same as always."

"You can't be." Eli shook his head firmly. "Daddy said today makes us a family. I got a daddy." He grinned at Gabe. "But I hafta have a mommy, too. My other mommy would be happy," he assured her seriously. "'Cause she loved me."

"So do I, Eli, and I would love to be your mommy.

Thank you." Tears filled her eyes at the wonderful gift of this little boy.

"You're a lucky kid to have the two best mommies in the world." Gabe swung his son into his arms, then threaded his other arm around Olivia's waist. "Now we're a family."

"Ladies and gentlemen, may I present Mr. and Mrs. Gabe Webber. And family," the pastor added, after Eli glowered at him.

The bride and groom laughed, hugged and enjoyed the afternoon. Though they were eager to be off on their short honeymoon, they were delayed by questions about their plans for the future.

"What will you do now?" people asked Gabe.

"Settle in to Trust Farms, that's the name of our spread. Keep working at the Double M and with the foster youth who come to The Haven for respite." He winked at Olivia. "In our spare time, I'll start a petting zoo with my wife and son and try to do whatever God asks of us."

Later, as they lifted off in an aircraft that would take them on their honeymoon to Maui, Olivia leaned her head against Gabe's shoulder.

"Aside from falling in love, getting married and finding your son, what's changed with us, Gabe?"

He thought for a minute.

"We've put the past in the past, where it belongs. Now we're focused on our future together, with God, whatever it is."

"Yeah." She smiled and nodded. "I finally figured it out."

Gabe arched an eyebrow, waiting.

"Home isn't where you are. It's who you're with."

"Now you're talking." He stole a kiss. Then she giggled.

"I forgot to ask if you liked your first wedding gift."

He patted his flat waist. "Love it, though I've never had a belt made of rope before."

"I'm thinking it might be a good craft when we're snowed in this winter. We always need a good craft to keep the kids busy."

They leaned back into their seats and began planning for their future.

Together.

* * * * *

If you enjoyed this story, pick up the first two
Rocky Mountain Haven books,

Meant-To-Be Baby
Mistletoe Twins

and these other stories from Lois Richer:

The Rancher's Family Wish
Her Christmas Family Wish
The Cowboy's Easter Family Wish
The Twins' Family Wish
A Dad for Her Twins
Rancher Daddy
Gift-Wrapped Family
Accidental Dad

Available now from Love Inspired!

Find more great reads at
www.LoveInspired.com.

Dear Reader,

Hello! Welcome back to my Rocky Mountain sanctuary, The Haven, a place of respite for foster children. I hope you enjoyed Olivia's journey to find out where she belonged, and Gabe's struggle to forgive when the cost was so great. And Eli's search—to find a home.

The past year has brought loss and birth to our family, struggles and blessings. And yet, God is always there for us to cast our cares on Him because He cares for us. I hope that you have found His solace in your life's journey. Please join me again soon for Gemma's story, the final book in this series.

I'd be delighted to hear from you via my website at www.loisricher.com, email at loisricher@gmail.com or by snail mail at Lois Richer, Box 639, Nipawin, Sask. Canada S0E 1E0. It's always a blessing to hear from readers and I'll do my best to respond quickly.

Until we meet again, may you know the everlasting love, joy and peace that God offers to all His children.

Blessings,
Lois Richer

COMING NEXT MONTH FROM
Love Inspired®

Available April 16, 2019

A PERFECT AMISH MATCH
Indiana Amish Brides • by Vannetta Chapman

Positive he's meant to stay a bachelor, Noah Graber enlists Amish matchmaker Olivia Mae Miller to set up three dates—and prove to his parents that relationships aren't for him. But when he starts falling for Olivia Mae, can they forget their reasons for *not* marrying and build a future together?

HER NEW AMISH FAMILY
Amish Country Courtships • by Carrie Lighte

Widower Seth Helmuth needs a mother for his little twin boys, but for now, he hires the *Englischer* temporarily living next door as their nanny. But while he searches for the perfect wife and mother, he can't help but think Trina Smith is the best fit...if only she were Amish.

HIS WYOMING BABY BLESSING
Wyoming Cowboys • by Jill Kemerer

When pregnant widow Kit McAllistor arrives at Wade Croft's ranch hoping to stay in one of his cabins, Wade can't turn away his childhood best friend—even if his ranch may soon be for sale. But he's determined to keep his feelings for Kit and her baby strictly friendship.

HER TWINS' COWBOY DAD
Montana Twins • by Patricia Johns

Colt Hardin's surprised to learn his uncle's will is more complicated than he expected—he'll inherit the ranch he was promised...but his late cousin's twin toddlers get the cattle. Can he keep an emotional distance from the children's mother, Jane Marshall, until his purchase of the cattle is finalized?

THE RANCHER'S REDEMPTION
by Myra Johnson

Including his property in the local historical society's grand tour could have huge benefits for Kent Ritter, but he has no clue how to decorate it. So he strikes a deal with town newcomer Erin Dearborn—she'll give him decorating advice if he'll make repairs to her home.

RESTORING HER FAITH
by Jennifer Slattery

Hired to restore the town's church, artist Faith Nichols must work with widowed contractor Drake Owens on the project. But as they collaborate to renovate the building, will Faith restore Drake's heart, as well?

LOOK FOR THESE AND OTHER LOVE INSPIRED BOOKS WHEREVER BOOKS ARE SOLD, INCLUDING MOST BOOKSTORES, SUPERMARKETS, DISCOUNT STORES AND DRUGSTORES.

LICNM0419

SPECIAL EXCERPT FROM

Love Inspired®

When a young Amish man needs help finding a wife, his beautiful matchmaker agrees to give him dating lessons…

Read on for a sneak preview of
A Perfect Amish Match *by Vannetta Chapman, available May 2019 from Love Inspired!*

"Dating is so complicated."

"People are complicated, Noah. Every single person you meet is dealing with something."

He asked, "How did you get so wise?"

"Never said I was."

"I'm being serious. How did you learn to navigate so seamlessly through these kinds of interactions, and why aren't you married?"

Olivia Mae thought her eyes were going to pop out of her head. "Did you really just ask me that?"

"I did."

"A little intrusive."

"Meaning you don't want to answer?"

"Meaning it's none of your business."

"Fair enough, though it's like asking a horse salesman why he doesn't own a horse."

"My family situation is…unique."

"You mean with your grandparents?"

She nodded instead of answering.

"I've got it." Noah resettled his hat, looking quite pleased with himself.

"Got what?"

"The solution to my dating disasters."

He leaned forward, close enough that she could smell the shampoo he'd used that morning.

"You need to give me dating lessons."

"What do you mean?"

"You and me. We'll go on a few dates…say, three. You can learn how to do anything if you do it three times."

"That's a ridiculous suggestion."

"Why? I learn better from doing."

"Do you?"

"I've already learned not to take a girl to a gas station, but who knows how many more dating traps are waiting for me."

"So this would be…a learning experience."

"It's a perfect solution." He tugged on her *kapp* string, something no one had done to her since she'd been a young teen.

"I can tell by the shock on your face that I've made you uncomfortable. It's a *gut* idea, though. We'd keep it businesslike— nothing personal."

Olivia Mae had no idea why the thought of sitting through three dates with Noah Graber made her stomach twirl like she'd been on a merry-go-round. Maybe she was catching a stomach bug.

"Wait a minute. Are you trying to get out of your third date? Because you promised your *mamm* that you would give this thing three solid attempts."

"And I'll keep my word on that," Noah assured her. "After you've tutored me, you can throw another poor unsuspecting girl my way."

Olivia Mae stood, brushed off the back of her dress and pointed a finger at Noah, who still sat in the grass as if he didn't have a care in the world.

"All right. I'll do it."

Don't miss
A Perfect Amish Match *by Vannetta Chapman,*
available May 2019 wherever
Love Inspired® books and ebooks are sold.

www.LoveInspired.com